VITTORIA
Book 2

By

GEORGE MEREDITH

Double 9 Books

Vittoria
Book 2

by **George Meredith**

ISBN: 978-93-57484-39-8

Published by

DOUBLE 9 BOOKS
2/13-B, Ansari Road, Daryaganj
New Delhi - 110002
info@double9books.com
www.double9books.com
Tel. 011-40042856

ABOUT THE AUTHOR

George Meredith OM (February 12, 1828-May 18, 1909) was born in Portsmouth, United Kingdom. He was an English poet, writer, and author, whose books are noted for their intelligence, extraordinary dialogues, and aphoristic way of writing. Meredith's books are also recognised for psychological studies of character and a highly subjective perspective on life that is a long way ahead of its time, considering women are equals to men in all streams. His most popular works are The Ordeal of Richard Feverel (1859) and The Egoist (1879). He was nominated for the Nobel Prize in Literature seven times.

CONTENTS

CHAPTER IX
IN VERONA

The lieutenant read these lines, as he clattered through the quiet streets toward the Porta Tosa:

'DEAR FRIEND,—I am glad that you remind me of our old affection, for it assures me that yours is not dead. I cannot consent to see you yet. I would rather that we should not meet.

'I thought I would sign my name here, and say, "God bless you, Wilfrid; go!"

'Oh! why have you done this thing! I must write on. It seems like my past life laughing at me, that my old friend should have come here in Italy, to wear the detestable uniform. How can we be friends when we must act as enemies? We shall soon be in arms, one against the other. I pity you, for you have chosen a falling side; and when you are beaten back, you can have no pride in your country, as we Italians have; no delight, no love. They will call you a mercenary soldier. I remember that I used to have the fear of your joining our enemies, when we were in England, but it seemed too much for my reason.

'You are with a band of butchers. If I could see you and tell you the story of Giacomo Piaveni, and some other things, I believe you would break your sword instantly.

'There is time. Come to Milan on the fifteenth. You will see me then. I appear at La Scala. Promise me, if you hear me, that you will do exactly what I make you feel it right to do. Ah, you will not, though thousands will! But step aside to me, when the curtain falls, and remain—oh, dear friend! I write in honour to you; we have sworn to free the city and the country—remain among us: break your sword, tear off your uniform; we are so strong that we are irresistible. I know what a hero you can be on the field: then, why not in the true cause?

I do not understand that you should waste your bravery under that ugly flag, bloody and past forgiveness.

'I shall be glad to have news of you all, and of England. The bearer of this is a trusty messenger, and will continue to call at the hotel. A. is offended that I do not allow my messenger to give my address; but I must not only be hidden, I must have peace, and forget you all until I have done my task. Addio. We have both changed names. I am the same. Can I think that you are? Addio, dear friend.

'VITTORIA.'

Lieutenant Pierson read again and again the letter of her whom he had loved in England, to get new lights from it, as lovers do when they have lost the power to take single impressions. He was the bearer of a verbal despatch from the commandant in Milan to the Marshal in Verona. At that period great favour was shown to Englishmen in the Austrian service, and the lieutenant's uncle being a General of distinction, he had a sort of semi-attachment to the Marshal's staff, and was hurried to and fro, for the purpose of keeping him out of duelling scrapes, as many of his friendlier comrades surmised. The right to the distinction of exercising staff-duties is, of course, only to be gained by stout competitorship in the Austrian service; but favour may do something for a young man even in that rigorous school of Arms. He had to turn to Brescia on his way, and calculated that if luck should put good horses under him, he would enter Verona gates about sunset. Meantime; there was Vittoria's letter to occupy him as he went.

We will leave him to his bronzing ride through the mulberries and the grapes, and the white and yellow and arid hues of the September plain, and make acquaintance with some of his comrades of that proud army which Vittoria thought would stand feebly against the pouring tide of Italian patriotism.

The fairest of the cities of the plain had long been a nest of foreign soldiery. The life of its beauty was not more visible then than now. Within the walls there are glimpses of it, that belong rather to the haunting spirit than to the life. Military science has made a mailed giant of Verona, and a silent one, save upon occasion. Its face grins of war, like a skeleton of death; the salient image of the skull and congregating worms was one that Italian lyrists applied naturally to Verona.

The old Field-Marshal and chief commander of the Austrian forces in Lombardy, prompted by the counsels of his sagacious adlatus, the chief of the staff, was engaged at that period in adding some of those ugly round walls and flanking bastions to Verona, upon which, when Austria was thrown back by the first outburst of the insurrection and the advance of the Piedmontese, she was enabled to plant a sturdy hind-foot, daring her foes as from a rock of defence.

A group of officers, of the cavalry, with a few infantry uniforms skirting them, were sitting in the pleasant cooling evening air, fanned by the fresh springing breeze, outside one of the Piazza Bra caffes, close upon the shadow of the great Verona amphitheatre. They were smoking their attenuated long straw cigars, sipping iced lemonade or coffee, and talking the common talk of the garrison officers, with perhaps that additional savour of a robust immorality which a Viennese social education may give. The rounded ball of the brilliant September moon hung still aloft, lighting a fathomless sky as well as the fair earth. It threw solid blackness from the old savage walls almost to a junction with their indolent outstretched feet. Itinerant street music twittered along the Piazza; officers walked arm-in-arm; now in moonlight bright as day, now in a shadow black as night: distant figures twinkled with the alternation. The light lay like a blade's sharp edge around the massive circle. Of Italians of a superior rank, Verona sent none to this resort. Even the melon-seller stopped beneath the arch ending the Stradone Porta Nuova, as if he had reached a marked limit of his popular customers.

This isolation of the rulers of Lombardy had commenced in Milan, but, owing to particular causes, was not positively defined there as it was in Verona. War was already rageing between the Veronese ladies and the officers of Austria. According to the Gallic Terpsichorean code, a lady who permits herself to make election of her partners and to reject applicants to the honour of her hand in the dance, when that hand is disengaged, has no just ground of complaint if a glove should smite her cheek. The Austrians had to endure this sort of rejection in Ballrooms. On the promenade their features were forgotten. They bowed to statues. Now, the officers of Austria who do not belong to a Croat regiment, or to one drawn from any point of the extreme East of the empire, are commonly gentlemanly men; and though they can be vindictive after much irritation, they may claim at least as good a reputation for forbearance in a conquered country as our officers in India. They are not ill-humoured, and they are not peevishly arrogant, except upon provocation. The conduct of the tender Italian dames was vexatious. It was exasperating to these knights of the slumbering sword to hear their native waltzes sounding of exquisite Vienna, while their legs stretched in melancholy inactivity on the Piazza pavement, and their arms encircled no ductile waists. They tried to despise it more than they disliked it, called their female foes Amazons, and their male by a less complimentary title, and so waited for the patriotic epidemic to pass.

A certain Captain Weisspriess, of the regiment named after a sagacious monarch whose crown was the sole flourishing blossom of diplomacy, particularly distinguished himself by insisting that a lady should remember him in public places. He was famous for skill with his weapons. He waltzed admirably; erect as under his Field-Marshal's eye. In the language of his brother officers, he was successful; that is, even as God Mars when Bellona does not rage. Captain Weisspriess (Johann Nepomuk, Freiherr von Scheppenhausen) resembled in appearance one in the Imperial Royal service, a gambling General of Division, for whom Fame had not yet blown her blast. Rumour declared that they might be relatives; a little- scrupulous society did not hesitate to mention how. The captain's moustache was straw-coloured; he wore it beyond the regulation length and caressed it infinitely. Surmounted by a pair of hot eyes, wavering in their direction, this grand moustache was a feature to be forgotten with difficulty, and Weisspriess was doubtless correct in asserting that his face had endured a slight equal to a buffet. He stood high and square- shouldered; the flame of the moustache streamed on either side his face in a splendid curve; his vigilant head was loftily posted to detect what he chose to construe as insult, or gather the smiles of approbation, to which, owing to the unerring judgement of the sex, he was more accustomed. Handsome or not, he enjoyed the privileges of masculine beauty.

This captain of a renown to come pretended that a superb Venetian lady of the Branciani family was bound to make response in public to his private signals, and publicly to reply to his salutations. He refused to be as a particle in space floating airily before her invincible aspect. Meeting her one evening, ere sweet Italy had exiled herself from the Piazza, he bowed, and stepping to the front of her, bowed pointedly. She crossed her arms and gazed over him. He called up a thing to her recollection in resonant speech. Shameful lie, or shameful truth, it was uttered in the hearing of many of his brother officers, of three Italian ladies, and of an Italian gentleman, Count Broncini, attending them. The lady listened calmly. Count Broncini smote him on the face. That evening the lady's brother arrived from Venice, and claimed his right to defend her. Captain Weisspriess ran him through the body, and attached a sinister label to his corpse. This he did not so much from brutality; the man felt that henceforth while he held his life he was at war with every Italian gentleman of mettle. Count Broncini was his next victim. There, for a time, the slaughtering business of the captain stopped. His brother officers of the better kind would not have excused him at another season, but the avenger of their irritation and fine vindicator of the merits of Austrian steel, had a welcome truly warm, when at the termination of his second duel he strode into mess, or what serves for an Austrian regimental mess.

It ensued naturally that there was everywhere in Verona a sharp division between the Italians of all classes and their conquerors. The great green-rinded melons were never wheeled into the neighbourhood of the whitecoats. Damsels were no longer coquettish under the military glance, but hurried by in couples; and there was much scowling mixed with derisive servility, throughout the city, hard to be endured without that hostile state of the spirit which is the military mind's refuge in such cases. Itinerant musicians, and none but this fry, continued to be attentive to the dispensers of soldi.

The Austrian army prides itself upon being a brotherhood. Discipline is very strict, but all commissioned officers, when off duty, are as free in their intercourse as big boys. The General accepts a cigar from the lieutenant, and in return lifts his glass to him. The General takes an interest in his lieutenant's love-affairs: nor is the latter shy when he feels it his duty modestly to compliment his superior officer upon a recent conquest. There is really good fellowship both among the officers and in the ranks, and it is systematically encouraged.

The army of Austria was in those days the Austrian Empire. Outside the army the empire was a jealous congery of intriguing disaffected nationalities. The same policy which played the various States against one another in order to reduce all to subserviency to the central Head, erected a privileged force wherein the sentiment of union was fostered till it became a nationality of the sword. Nothing more fatal can be done for a country; but for an army it is a simple measure of wisdom. Where the password is MARCH, and not DEVELOP, a body of men, to be a serviceable instrument, must consent to act as one. Hannibal is the historic example of what a General can accomplish with tribes who are thus, enrolled in a new citizenship; and (as far as we know of him and his fortunes) he appears to be an example of the necessity of the fusing fire of action to congregated aliens in arms. When Austria was fighting year after year, and being worsted in campaign after campaign, she lost foot by foot, but she held together soundly; and more than the baptism, the atmosphere of strife has always been required to give her a healthy vitality as a centralized empire. She knew it; this (apart from the famous promptitude of the Hapsburgs) was one secret of her dauntless readiness to fight. War did the work of a smithy for the iron and steel holding her together; and but that war costs money, she would have been an empire distinguished by aggressiveness. The next best medicinal thing to war is the military occupation of insurgent provinces. The soldiery soon feel where their home is, and feel the pride of atomies in unitive power, when they are sneered at, hooted, pelted, stabbed upon a gross misinterpretation of the slightest of moral offences, shamefully abused for doing their duty with a considerate sense of it, and too accurately divided from the inhabitants of the land they hold. In Italy, the German, the Czech, the Magyar, the Croft, even in general instances the Italian, clung to the standard for safety, for pay, for glory, and all became pre-eminently Austrian soldiers; little besides.

It was against a power thus bound in iron hoops, that Italy, dismembered, and jealous, and corrupt, with an organization promoted by passion chiefly, was preparing to rise. In the end, a country true to itself and determined to claim God's gift to brave men will overmatch a mere army, however solid its force. But an inspired energy of faith is demanded of it. The intervening chapters will show pitiable weakness, and such a schooling of disaster as makes men, looking on the surface of things, deem the struggle folly. As well, they might say, let yonder scuffling vagabonds up any of the Veronese side-streets fall upon the patrol marching like one man, and hope to overcome them! In Vienna there was often despair: but it never existed in the Austrian camp. Vienna was frequently double-dealing and time-serving her force in arms was like a trained man feeling his muscle. Thus, when the Government thought of temporizing, they issued orders to Generals whose one idea was to strike the blow of a mallet.

At this period there was no suspicion of any grand revolt being in process of development. The abounding dissatisfaction was treated as nothing more than the Italian disease showing symptoms here and there, and Vienna counselled measures mildly repressive,—'conciliating,' it was her pleasure to call them. Her recent commands with respect to turbulent Venice were the subject of criticism among the circle outside the Piazza Gaffe. An enforced inactivity of the military legs will quicken the military wits, it would appear, for some of the younger officers spoke hotly as to their notion of the method of ruling Venezia. One had bidden his Herr General to 'look here,' while he stretched forth his hand and declared that Italians were like women, and wanted—yes, wanted—(their instinct called for it) a beating, a real beating; as the emphatic would say in our vernacular, a thundering thrashing, once a month:-'Or so,' the General added acquiescingly. A thundering thrashing, once a month or so, to these unruly Italians, because they are like women! It was a youth who spoke, but none doubted his acquaintance with women, or cared to suggest that his education in that department of knowledge was an insufficient guarantee for his fitness to govern Venezia. Two young dragoon officers had approached during the fervid allocution, and after the salute to their superior, caught up chairs and stamped them down, thereupon calling for the loan of anybody's cigar-case. Where it is that an Austrian officer ordinarily keeps this instrument so necessary to his comfort, and obnoxious, one would suppose, to the rigid correctness of his shapely costume, we cannot easily guess. None can tell even where he stows away his pocket-handkerchief, or haply his purse. However, these things appear on demand. Several elongated cigar-cases were thrust forward, and then it was seen that the attire of the gallant youngsters was in disorder.

'Did you hunt her to earth?' they were asked.

The reply trenched on philosophy; and consisted in an inquiry as to who cared for the whole basketful—of the like description of damsels, being implied. Immoderate and uproarious laughter burst around them. Both seemed to have been clawed impartially. Their tightfitting coats bulged at the breast or opened at the waist, as though buttons were lacking, and the whiteness of that garment cried aloud for the purification of pipeclay. Questions flew. The damsel who had been pursued was known as a pretty girl, the daughter of a blacksmith, and no prolonged resistance was expected from one of her class. But, as it came out, she had said, a week past, 'I shall be stabbed if I am seen talking to you'; and therefore the odd matter was, not that she had, in tripping down the Piazza with her rogue-eyed cousin from Milan, looked away and declined all invitation to moderate her pace and to converse, but that, after doubling down and about lonely streets, the length of which she ran as swiftly as her feet would carry her, at a corner of the Via Colomba she allowed herself to be caught—wilfully, beyond a doubt, seeing that she was not a bit breathed—allowed one quick taste of her lips, and then shrieked as naturally as a netted bird, and brought a hustling crowd just at that particular point to her rescue: not less than fifty, and all men. 'Not a woman among them!' the excited young officer repeated.

A veteran in similar affairs could see that he had the wish to remain undisturbed in his bewilderment at the damsel's conduct. Profound belief in her partiality for him perplexed his recent experience rather agreeably. Indeed, it was at this epoch an article of faith with the Austrian military that nothing save terror of their males kept sweet Italian women from the expression of their preference for the broad-shouldered, thick-limbed, yellow-haired warriors—the contrast to themselves which is supposed greatly to inspirit genial Cupid in the selection from his quiver.

'What became of her? Did you let her go?' came pestering remarks, too absurd for replies if they had not been so persistent.

'Let her go? In the devil's name, how was I to keep my hold of her in a crowd of fifty of the fellows, all mowing, and hustling, and elbowing— every rascal stinking right under my nose like the pit?'

''Hem!' went the General present. 'As long as you did not draw! Unsheathe, a minute.'

He motioned for a sight of their naked swords.

The couple of young officers flushed.

'Herr General! Pardon!' they remonstrated.

'No, no. I know how boys talk; I've been one myself. Tutt! You tell the truth, of course; but the business is for me to know in what! how far! Your swords, gentlemen.'

'But, General!'

'Well? I merely wish to examine the blades.'

'Do you doubt our words?'

'Hark at them! Words? Are you lawyers? A soldier deals in acts. I don't want to know your words, but your deeds, my gallant lads. I want to look at the blades of your swords, my children. What was the last order? That on no account were we to provoke, or, if possibly to be avoided, accept a collision, etc., etc. The soldier in peace is a citizen, etc. No sword on any account, or for any excuse, to be drawn, etc. You all heard it? So, good! I receive your denial, my children. In addition, I merely desire to satisfy curiosity. Did the guard clear a way for you?'

The answer was affirmative.

'Your swords!'

One of them drew, and proffered the handle.

The other clasped the haft angrily, and with a resolute smack on it, settled it in the scabbard.

'Am I a prisoner, General?'

'Not at all!'

'Then I decline to surrender my sword.'

Another General officer happened to be sauntering by. Applauding with his hands, and choosing the Italian language as the best form of speech for the enunciation of ironical superlatives, he said:

'Eccellentemente! most admirable! of a distinguished loftiness of moral grandeur: "Then I decline," etc.: you are aware that you are quoting? "as the drummerboy said to Napoleon." I think you forgot to add that? It is the same young soldier who utters these immense things, which we can hardly get out of our mouths. So the little fellow towers! His moral greatness is as noisy as his drum. What's wrong?'

'General Pierson, nothing's wrong,' was replied by several voices; and some explained that Lieutenant Jenna had been called upon by General Schoneck to show his sword, and had refused.

The heroic defender of his sword shouted to the officer with whom General
Pierson had been conversing: 'Here! Weisspriess!'

'What is it, my dear fellow? Speak, my good Jenna!'

The explanation was given, and full sympathy elicited from Captain Weisspriess, while the two Generals likewise whispered and nodded.

'Did you draw?' the captain inquired, yawning. 'You needn't say it in quite so many words, if you did. I shall be asked by the General presently; and owing to that duel pending 'twixt you and his nephew, of which he is aware, he may put a bad interpretation on your pepperiness.'

'The devil fetch his nephew!' returned the furious Lieutenant Jenna. 'He comes back to-night from Milan, and if he doesn't fight me to-morrow, I post him a coward. Well, about that business! My good Weisspriess, the fellows had got into a thick crowd all round, and had begun to knead me. Do you understand me? I felt their knuckles.'

'Ah, good, good!' said the captain. 'Then, you didn't draw, of course. What officer of the Imperial service would, under similar circumstances! That is my reply to the Emperor, if ever I am questioned. To draw would be to show that an Austrian officer relies on his good sword in the thick of his enemies; against which, as you know, my Jenna, the Government have issued an express injunction button. Did you sell it dear?'

'A fellow parted with his ear for it.'

Lieutenant Jenna illustrated a particular cut from a turn of his wrist.

'That oughtn't to make a noise?' he queried somewhat anxiously.

'It won't hear one any longer, at all events,' said Captain Weisspriess; and the two officers entered into the significance of the remark with enjoyment.

Meantime General Pierson had concluded an apparently humorous dialogue with his brother General, and the later, now addressing Lieutenant Jenna, said: 'Since you prefer surrendering your person rather than your sword— it is good! Report yourself at the door of my room to-night, at ten. I suspect that you have been blazing your steel, sir. They say, 'tis as ready to flash out as your temper.'

Several voices interposed: 'General! what if he did draw!'

'Silence. You have read the recent order. Orlando may have his Durindarda bare; but you may not. Grasp that fact. The Government wish to make Christians of you, my children. One cheek being smitten, what should you do?'

'Shall I show you, General?' cried a quick little subaltern.

'The order, my children, as received a fortnight since from our old Wien, commands you to offer the other cheek to the smiter.'

'So that a proper balance may be restored to both sides of the face,' General Pierson appended.

'And mark me,' he resumed. 'There may be doubts about the policy of anything, though I shouldn't counsel you to cherish them: but there's no mortal doubt about the punishment for this thing.' The General spoke sternly; and then relaxing the severity of his tone, he said, 'The desire of the Government is to make an army of Christians.'

'And a precious way of doing it!' interjected two or three of the younger officers. They perfectly understood how hateful the Viennese domination was to their chiefs, and that they would meet sympathy and tolerance for any extreme of irony, provided that they showed a disposition to be subordinate. For the bureaucratic order, whatever it was, had to be obeyed. The army might, and of course did, know best: nevertheless it was bound to be nothing better than a machine in the hands of the dull closeted men in Vienna, who judged of difficulties and plans of action from a calculation of numbers, or from foreign journals—from heaven knows what!

General Schoneck and General Pierson walked away laughing, and the younger officers were left to themselves. Half-a-dozen of them interlaced arms, striding up toward the Porta Nuova, near which, at the corner of the Via Trinita, they had the pleasant excitement of beholding a riderless horse suddenly in mid gallop sink on its knees and roll over. A crowd came pouring after it, and from the midst the voice of a comrade hailed them. 'It's Pierson,' cried Lieutenant Jenna. The officers drew their swords, and hailed the guard from the gates.

Lieutenant Pierson dropped in among their shoulders, dead from want of breath. They held him up, and finding him sound, thumped his back. The blade of his sword was red. He coughed with their thumpings, and sang out to them to cease; the idle mob which had been at his heels drew back before the guard could come up with them. Lieutenant Pierson gave no explanation except that he had been attacked near Juliet's tomb on his way to General Schoneck's quarters. Fellows had stabbed his horse, and brought him to the ground, and torn the coat off his back. He complained in bitter mutterings of the loss of a letter therein, during the first candid moments of his anger: and, as he was known to be engaged to the Countess Lena von Lenkenstein, it was conjectured by his comrades that this lady might have had something to do with the ravishment of the letter. Great laughter surrounded him, and he looked from man to man. Allowance is naturally made for the irascibility of a brother officer coming tattered out of the hands of enemies, or Lieutenant Jenna would have construed his eye's challenge on the spot. As it was, he cried out, 'The letter! the letter! Charge, for the honour of the army, and rescue the letter!' Others echoed him: 'The letter! the letter! the English letter!' A foreigner in an army can have as much provocation as he pleases; if he is anything of a favourite with his superiors, his fellows will task his forbearance. Wilfrid Pierson glanced at the blade of his sword, and slowly sheathed it. 'Lieutenant Jenna is a good actor before a mob,' he said. 'Gentlemen, I rely upon you to make no noise about that letter; it is a private matter. In an hour or so, if any officer shall choose to question me concerning it, I will answer him.'

The last remnants of the mob had withdrawn. The officer in command at the gates threw a cloak over Wilfrid's shoulders; and taking the arm of a friend Wilfrid hurried to barracks, and was quickly in a position to report himself to his General, whose first remark, 'Has the dead horse been removed?' robbed him of his usual readiness to equivocate. 'When you are the bearer of a verbal despatch, come straight to quarters, if you have to come like a fig-tree on the north side of the wall in Winter,' said General Schoneck, who was joined presently by General Pierson.

'What 's this I hear of some letter you have been barking about all over the city?' the latter asked, after returning his nephew's on-duty salute.

Wilfrid replied that it was a letter of his sister's treating of family matters.

The two Generals, who were close friends, discussed the attack to which he had been subjected. Wilfrid had to recount it with circumstance: how, as he was nearing General Schoneck's quarters at a military trot, six men headed by a leader had dashed out on him from a narrow side-street, unhorsed him after a struggle, rifled the saddlebags, and torn the coat from his back, and had taken the mark of his sword, while a gathering crowd looked on, hooting. His horse had fled, and he confessed that he had followed his horse. General Schoneck spoke the name of Countess Lena suggestively. 'Not a bit,' returned General Pierson; 'the fellow courts her too hotly. The scoundrels here want a bombardment; that 's where it lies. A dose of iron pills will make Verona a healthy place. She must have it.'

General Schoneck said, 'I hope not,' and laughed at the heat of Irish blood. He led Wilfrid in to the Marshal, after which Wilfrid was free to seek Lieutenant Jenna, who had gained the right to a similar freedom by pledging his honour not to fight within a stipulated term of days. The next morning Wilfrid was roused by an orderly coming from his uncle, who placed in his hands a copy of Vittoria's letter: at the end of it his uncle had written, 'Rather astonishing. Done pretty well; but by a foreigner. "Affection" spelt with one "f." An Italian: you will see the letters are emphatic at "ugly flag"; also "bloody and past forgiveness" very large; the copyist had a dash of the feelings of a commentator, and did his (or her) best to add an oath to it. Who the deuce, sir, is this opera girl calling herself Vittoria? I have a lecture for you. German women don't forgive diversions during courtship; and if you let this Countess Lena slip, your chance has gone. I compliment you on your power of lying; but you must learn to show your right face to me, or the very handsome feature, your nose, and that useful box, your skull, will come to grief. The whole business is a mystery. The letter (copy) was directed to you, brought to me, and opened in a fit of abstraction, necessary to commanding uncles who are trying to push the fortunes of young noodles pretending to be related to them. Go to Countess Lena. Count Paul is with her, from Bologna. Speak to her, and observe her and him. He knows English—has been attached to the embassy in London; but, pooh! the hand's Italian. I confess myself puzzled. We shall possibly have to act on the intimation of the fifteenth, and profess to be wiser than others. Something is brewing for business. See Countess Lena boldly, and then come and breakfast with me.'

Wilfrid read the miserable copy of Vittoria's letter, utterly unable to resolve anything in his mind, except that he would know among a thousand the leader of those men who had attacked him, and who bore the mark of his sword.

CHAPTER X
THE POPE'S MOUTH

Barto Rizzo had done what he had sworn to do. He had not found it difficult to outstrip the lieutenant (who had to visit Brescia on his way) and reach the gates of Verona in advance of him, where he obtained entrance among a body of grape-gatherers and others descending from the hills to meet a press of labour in the autumnal plains. With them he hoped to issue forth unchallenged on the following morning; but Wilfrid's sword had made lusty play; and, as in the case when the order has been given that a man shall be spared in life and limb, Barto and his fellow- assailants suffered by their effort to hold him simply half a minute powerless. He received a shrewd cut across the head, and lay for a couple of hours senseless in the wine-shop of one Battista—one of the many all over Lombardy who had pledged their allegiance to the Great Cat, thinking him scarcely vulnerable. He read the letter, dizzy with pain, and with the frankness proper to inflated spirits after loss of blood, he owned to himself that it was not worth much as a prize. It was worth the attempt to get possession of it, for anything is worth what it costs, if it be only as a schooling in resolution, energy, and devotedness:—regrets are the sole admission of a fruitless business; they show the bad tree;—so, according to his principle of action, he deliberated; but he was compelled to admit that Vittoria's letter was little else than a repetition of her want of discretion when she was on the Motterone. He admitted it, wrathfully: his efforts to convict this woman telling him she deserved some punishment; and his suspicions being unsatisfied, he resolved to keep them hungry upon her, and return to Milan at once. As to the letter itself, he purposed, since the harm in it was accomplished, to send it back honourably to the lieutenant, till finding it blood- stained, he declined to furnish the gratification of such a sight to any Austrian sword. For that reason, he copied it, while Battista's wife held double bandages tight round his head: believing that the letter stood transcribed in a precisely similar hand, he forwarded it to Lieutenant Pierson, and then sank and swooned. Two days he lay incapable and let his thoughts dance as they would. Information was brought to him that the gates were strictly watched, and that troops were starting for Milan. This was in the dull hour antecedent to the dawn. 'She is a traitress!' he exclaimed, and leaping from his bed, as with a brain striking fire, screamed, 'Traitress! traitress!' Battista and his wife had to fling themselves on him and gag him, guessing him as mad. He spoke pompously and theatrically; called himself the Eye of Italy, and said that he must be in Milan, or Milan would perish, because of the traitress: all with a great sullen air of composure and an odd distension of the eyelids. When they released him, he smiled and thanked them, though they knew, that had he chosen, he could have thrown off a dozen of them, such was his strength. The woman went down on her knees to him to get his consent that she should dress and bandage his head afresh. The sound of the regimental bugles drew him from the house, rather than any immediate settled scheme to watch at the gates.

Artillery and infantry were in motion before sunrise, from various points of the city, bearing toward the Palio and Zeno gates, and the people turned out to see them, for it was a march that looked like the beginning of things. The soldiers had green twigs in their hats, and kissed their hands good-humouredly to the gazing crowd, shouting bits of verses:

'I'm off! I'm off! Farewell, Mariandl! if I come back a sergeant-major or a Field-Marshal, don't turn up your nose at me: Swear you will be faithful all the while; because, when a woman swears, it's a comfort, somehow: Farewell! Squeeze the cow's udders: I shall be thirsty enough: You pretty wriggler! don't you know, the first cup of wine and the last, I shall float your name on it? Luck to the lads we leave behind! Farewell, Mariandl!'

The kindly fellows waved their hands and would take no rebuff. The soldiery of Austria are kindlier than most, until their blood is up. A Tyrolese regiment passed, singing splendidly in chorus. Songs of sentiment prevailed, but the traditions of a soldier's experience of the sex have informed his ballads with strange touches of irony, that help him to his (so to say) philosophy, which is recklessness. The Tyroler's

'Katchen' here, was a saturnine Giulia, who gave him no response, either of eye or lip.

'Little mother, little sister, little sweetheart, 'ade! ade!' My little sweetheart, your meadow is half-way up the mountain; it's such a green spot on the eyeballs of a roving boy! and the chapel just above it, I shall see it as I've seen it a thousand times; and the cloud hangs near it, and moves to the door and enters, for it is an angel, not a cloud; a white angel gone in to pray for Katerlein and me: Little mother, little sister, little sweetheart, 'ade! ade!' Keep single, Katerlein, as long as you can: as long as you can hold out, keep single: 'ade!''

Fifteen hundred men and six guns were counted as they marched on to one gate.

Barto Rizzo, with Battista and his wife on each side of him, were among the spectators. The black cock's feathers of the Tyrolese were still fluttering up the Corso, when the woman said, 'I 've known the tail of a regiment get through the gates without having to show paper.'

Battista thereupon asked Barto whether he would try that chance. The answer was a vacuous shake of the head, accompanied by an expression of unutterable mournfulness. 'There's no other way,' pursued Battista, 'unless you jump into the Adige, and swim down half-a-mile under water; and cats hate water—eh, my comico?'

He conceived that the sword-cut had rendered Barto imbecile, and pulled his hat down his forehead, and patted his shoulder, and bade him have cheer, patronizingly: but women do not so lightly lose their impression of a notable man. His wife checked him. Barto had shut his eyes, and hung swaying between them, as in drowsiness or drunkenness. Like his body, his faith was swaying within him. He felt it borne upon the reeling brain, and clung to it desperately, calling upon chance to aid him; for he was weak, incapable of a physical or mental contest, and this part of his settled creed that human beings alone failed the patriotic cause as instruments, while circumstances constantly befriended it—was shocked by present events. The image of Vittoria, the traitress, floated over the soldiery marching on Milan through her treachery. Never had an Austrian force seemed to him so terrible. He had to yield the internal fight, and let his faith sink and be blackened, in order that his mind might rest supine, according to his remembered system; for the inspiration which points to the right course does not come during mental strife, but after it, when faith summons its agencies undisturbed—if only men will have the faith, and will teach themselves to know that the inspiration must come, and will counsel them justly. This was a part of Barto Rizzo's sustaining creed; nor did he lose his grasp of it in the torment and the darkness of his condition.

He heard English voices. A carriage had stopped almost in front of him. A General officer was hat in hand, talking to a lady, who called him uncle, and said that she had been obliged to decide to quit Verona on account of her husband, to whom the excessive heat was unendurable. Her husband, in the same breath, protested that the heat killed him. He adorned the statement with all kinds of domestic and subterranean imagery, and laughed faintly, saying that after the fifteenth—on which night his wife insisted upon going to the Opera at Milan to hear a new singer and old friend—he should try a week at the Baths of Bormio, and only drop from the mountains when a proper temperature reigned, he being something of an invalid.

'And, uncle, will you be in Milan on the fifteenth?' said the lady; 'and Wilfrid, too?'

'Wilfrid will reach Milan as soon as you do, and I shall undoubtedly be there on the fifteenth,' said the General.

'I cannot possibly express to you how beautiful I think your army looks,' said the lady.

'Fine men, General Pierson, very fine men. I never saw such marching— equal to our Guards,' her husband remarked.

The lady named her Milanese hotel as the General waved his plumes, nodded, and rode off.

Before the carriage had started, Barto Rizzo dashed up to it; and 'Dear good English lady,' he addressed her, 'I am the brother of Luigi, who carries letters for you in Milan—little Luigi!—and I have a mother dying in Milan; and here I am in Verona, ill, and can't get to her, poor soul! Will you allow me that I may sit up behind as quiet as a mouse, and be near one of the lovely English ladies who are so kind to unfortunate persons, and never deaf to the name of charity? It's my mother who is dying, poor soul!'

The lady consulted her husband's face, which presented the total blank of one who refused to be responsible for an opinion hostile to the claims of charity, while it was impossible for him to fall in with foreign habits of familiarity, and accede to extraordinary petitions. Barto sprang up. 'I shall be your courier, dear lady,' he said, and commenced his professional career in her service by shouting to the vetturino to drive on. Wilfrid met them as he was trotting down from the Porta del Palio, and to him his sister confided her new trouble in having a strange man attached to her, who might be anything. 'We don't know the man,' said her husband; and Adela pleaded for him: 'Don't speak to him harshly, pray, Wilfrid; he says he has a mother dying in Milan.' Barto kept his head down on his arms and groaned; Adela gave a doleful little grimace. 'Oh, take the poor beggar,' said Wilfrid; and sang out to him in Italian: 'Who are you—what are you, my fine fellow?' Barto groaned louder, and replied in Swiss-French from a smothering depth: 'A poor man, and the gracious lady's servant till we reach Milan.'

'I can't wait,' said Wilfrid; 'I start in half-an-hour. It's all right; you must take him now you've got him, or else pitch him out—one of the two. If things go on quietly we shall have the Autumn manoeuvres in a week, and then you may see something of the army.' He rode away. Barto passed the gates as one of the licenced English family.

Milan was more strictly guarded than when he had quitted it. He had anticipated that it would be so, and tamed his spirit to submit to the slow stages of the carriage, spent a fiery night in Brescia, and entered the city of action on the noon of the fourteenth. Safe within the walls, he thanked the English lady, assuring her that her charitable deed would be remembered aloft. He then turned his steps in the direction of the Revolutionary post-office. This place was nothing other than a blank abutment of a corner house that had long been undergoing repair, and had a great bank of brick and mortar rubbish at its base. A stationary melonseller and some black fig and vegetable stalls occupied the triangular space fronting it. The removal of a square piece of cement showed a recess, where, chiefly during the night, letters and proclamation papers were deposited, for the accredited postman to disperse them. Hither, as one would go to a caffe for the news, Barto Rizzo came in the broad glare of noon, and flinging himself down like a tired man under the strip of shade, worked with a hand behind him, and drew out several folded scraps, of which one was addressed to him by his initials. He opened it and read:

'Your house is watched.

'A corporal of the P . . . ka regiment was seen leaving it this morning in time for the second bugle.

'Reply:—where to meet.

'Spies are doubled, troops coming.

'The numbers in Verona; who heads them.

'Look to your wife.

'Letters are called for every third hour.'

Barto sneered indolently at this fresh evidence of the small amount of intelligence which he could ever learn from others. He threw his eyes all round the vacant space while pencilling in reply:—

'V. waits for M., but in a box' (that is, Verona for Milan).

'We take the key to her.

'I have no wife, but a little pupil.

'A Lieutenant Pierson, of the dragoons; Czech white coats, helmets without plumes; an Englishman, nephew of General Pierson: speaks crippled Italian; returns from V. to-day. Keep eye on him;—what house, what hour.'

Meditating awhile, Barto wrote out Vittoria's name and enclosed it in a thick black ring.

Beneath it he wrote

'The same on all the play-bills.

'The Fifteenth is cancelled.

'We meet the day after.

'At the house of Count M. to-night.'

He secreted this missive, and wrote Vittoria's name on numbers of slips to divers addresses, heading them, 'From the Pope's Mouth,' such being the title of the Revolutionary postoffice, to whatsoever spot it might in prudence shift. The title was entirely complimentary to his Holiness. Tangible freedom, as well as airy blessings, were at that time anticipated, and not without warrant, from the mouth of the successor of St. Peter. From the Pope's Mouth the clear voice of Italian liberty was to issue. This sentiment of the period was a natural and a joyful one, and endowed the popular ebullition with a sense of unity and a stamp of righteousness that the abstract idea of liberty could not assure to it before martyrdom. After suffering, after walking in the shades of death and despair, men of worth and of valour cease to take high personages as representative objects of worship, even when these (as the good Pope was then doing) benevolently bless the nation and bid it to have great hope, with a voice of authority. But, for an extended popular movement a great name is like a consecrated banner. Proclamations from the Pope's Mouth exacted reverence, and Barto Rizzo, who despised the Pope (because he was Pope, doubtless), did not hesitate to make use of him by virtue of his office.

Barto lay against the heap of rubbish, waiting for the approach of his trained lad, Checco, a lanky simpleton, cunning as a pure idiot, who was doing postman's duty, when a kick, delivered by that youth behind, sent him bounding round with rage, like a fish in air. The marketplace resounded with a clapping of hands; for it was here that Checco came daily to eat figs, and it was known that the 'povero,' the dear half- witted creature, would not tolerate an intruder in the place where he stretched his limbs to peel and suck in the gummy morsels twice or thrice a day. Barto seized and shook him. Checco knocked off his hat; the bandage about the wound broke and dropped, and Barto put his hand to his forehead, murmuring: 'What 's come to me that I lose my temper with a boy—an animal?'

The excitement all over the triangular space was hushed by an imperious guttural shout that scattered the groups. Two Austrian officers, followed by military servants, rode side by side. Dust had whitened their mustachios, and the heat had laid a brown-red varnish on their faces. Way was made for them, while Barto stood smoothing his forehead and staring at Checco.

'I see the very man!' cried one of the officers quickly. 'Weisspriess, there's the rascal who headed the attack on me in Verona the other day. It's the same!

'Himmel!' returned his companion, scrutinizing the sword-cut, 'if that's your work on his head, you did it right well, my Pierson! He is very neatly scored indeed. A clean stroke, manifestly!'

'But here when I left Milan! at Verona when I entered the North-west gate there; and the first man I see as I come back is this very brute. He dogs me everywhere! By the way, there may be two of them.'

Lieutenant Pierson leaned over his horse's neck, and looked narrowly at the man Barto Rizzo. He himself was eyed as in retort, and with yet greater intentness. At first Barto's hand was sweeping the air within a finger's length of his forehead, like one who fought a giddiness for steady sight. The mist upon his brain dispersing under the gaze of his enemy, his eyeballs fixed, and he became a curious picture of passive malice, his eyes seeming to say: 'It is enough for me to know your features, and I know them.' Such a look from a civilian is exasperating: it was scarcely to be endured from an Italian of the plebs.

'You appear to me to want more,' said the lieutenant audibly to himself; and he repeated words to the same effect to his companion, in bad German.

'Eh? You would promote him to another epaulette?' laughed Captain Weisspriess. 'Come off. Orders are direct against it. And we're in Milan—not like being in Verona! And my good fellow! remember your bet; the dozen of iced Rudesheimer. I want to drink my share, and dream I'm quartered in Mainz—the only place for an Austrian when he quits Vienna. Come.'

'No; but if this is the villain who attacked me, and tore my coat from my back,' cried Wilfrid, screwing in his saddle.

'And took your letter took your letter; a particular letter; we have heard of it,' said Weisspriess.

The lieutenant exclaimed that he should overhaul and examine the man, and see whether he thought fit to give him into custody. Weisspriess laid hand on his bridle.

'Take my advice, and don't provoke a disturbance in the streets. The truth is, you Englishmen and Irishmen get us a bad name among these natives. If this is the man who unhorsed you and maltreated you, and committed the rape of the letter, I'm afraid you won't get satisfaction out of him, to judge by his look. I'm really afraid not. Try it if you like. In any case, if you halt, I am compelled to quit your society, which is sometimes infinitely diverting. Let me remind you that you bear despatches. The other day they were verbal ones; you are now carrying paper.'

'Are you anxious to teach me my duty, Captain Weisspriess?'

'If you don't know it. I said I would "remind you." I can also teach you, if you need it.'

'And I can pay you for the instruction, whenever you are disposed to receive payment.'

'Settle your outstanding claims, my good Pierson!'

'When I have fought Jenna?'

'Oh! you're a Prussian—a Prussian!' Captain Weisspriess laughed. 'A Prussian, I mean, in your gross way of blurting out everything. I've marched and messed with Prussians—with oxen.'

'I am, as you are aware, an Englishman, Captain Weisspriess. I am due to Lieutenant Jenna for the present. After that you or any one may command me.'

'As you please,' said Weisspriess, drawing out one stream of his moustache. 'In the meantime, thank me for luring you away from the chances of a street row.'

Barto Rizzo was left behind, and they rode on to the Duomo. Glancing up at its pinnacles, Weisspriess said:

'How splendidly Flatschmann's jagers would pick them off from there, now, if the dogs were giving trouble in this part of the city!'

They entered upon a professional discussion of the ways and means of dealing with a revolutionary movement in the streets of a city like Milan, and passed on to the Piazza La Scala. Weisspriess stopped before the Play-bills. 'To-morrow's the fifteenth of the month,' he said. 'Shall I tell you a secret, Pierson? I am to have a private peep at the new prima donna this night. They say she's charming, and very pert. "I do not interchange letters with Germans." Benlomik sent her a neat little note to the conservatorio—he hadn't seen her only heard of her, and that was our patriotic reply. She wants taming. I believe I am called upon for that duty. At least, my friend Antonio-Pericles, who occasionally assists me with supplies, hints as much to me. You're an engaged man, or, upon my honour, I wouldn't trust you; but between ourselves, this Greek—and he's quite right—is trying to get her away from the set of snuffy vagabonds who are prompting her for mischief, and don't know how to treat her.'

While he was speaking Barto Rizzo pushed roughly between them, and with a black brush painted the circle about Vittoria's name.

'Do you see that?' said Weisspriess.

'I see,' Wilfrid retorted, 'that you are ready to meddle with the reputation of any woman who is likely to be talked about. Don't do it in my presence.'

It was natural for Captain Weisspriess to express astonishment at this outburst, and the accompanying quiver of Wilfrid's lip.

'Austrian military etiquette, Lieutenant Pierson,' he said, 'precludes the suspicion that the officers of the Imperial army are subject to dissension in public. We conduct these affairs upon a different principle. But I'll tell you what. That fellow's behaviour may be construed as a more than common stretch of incivility. I'll do you a service. I'll arrest him, and then you can hear tidings of your precious letter. We'll have his confession published.'

Weisspriess drew his sword, and commanded the troopers in attendance to lay hands on Barto; but the troopers called, and the officer found that they were surrounded. Weisspriess shrugged dismally. 'The brute must go, I suppose,' he said. The situation was one of those which were every now and then occurring in the Lombard towns and cities, when a chance provocation created a riot that became a revolt or not, according to the timidity of the ruling powers or the readiness of the disaffected. The extent and evident regulation of the crowd operated as a warning to the Imperial officers. Weisspriess sheathed his sword and shouted, 'Way, there!' Way was made for him; but Wilfrid lingered to scrutinize the man who, for an unaccountable reason, appeared to be his peculiar enemy. Barto carelessly threaded the crowd, and Wilfrid, finding it useless to get out after him, cried, 'Who is he? Tell me the name of that man?' The question drew a great burst of laughter around him, and exclamations of 'Englishman! Englishman!' He turned where there was a clear way left for him in the track of his brother officer.

Comments on the petty disturbance had been all the while passing at the Caffe La Scala, where sat Agostino Balderini, with, Count Medole and others, who, if the order for their arrest had been issued, were as safe in that place as in their own homes. Their policy, indeed, was to show themselves openly abroad. Agostino was enjoying the smoke of paper cigarettes, with all prudent regard for the well-being of an inflammable beard. Perceiving Wilfrid going by, he said, 'An

Englishman! I continue to hope much from his countrymen. I have no right to do so, only they insist on it. They have promised, and more than once, to sail a fleet to our assistance across the plains of Lombardy, and I believe they will —probably in the watery epoch which is to follow Metternich. Behold my Carlo approaching. The heart of that lad doth so boil the brain of him, he can scarcely keep the lid on. What is it now? Speak, my son.'

Carlo Ammiani had to communicate that he had just seen a black circle to Vittoria's name on two public playbills. His endeavour to ape a deliberate gravity while he told the tale, roused Agostino's humouristic ire.

'Round her name?' said Agostino.

'Yes; in every bill.'

'Meaning that she is suspected!'

'Meaning any damnable thing you like.'

'It's a device of the enemy.'

Agostino, glad of the pretext to recur to his habitual luxurious irony, threw himself back, repeating 'It 's a device of the enemy. Calculate, my son, that the enemy invariably knows all you intend to do: determine simply to astonish him with what you do. Intentions have lungs, Carlo, and depend on the circumambient air, which, if not designedly treacherous, is communicative. Deeds, I need not remark, are a different body. It has for many generations been our Italian error to imagine a positive blood relationship—not to say maternity itself—existing between intentions and deeds. Nothing of the sort! There is only the intention of a link to unite them. You perceive? It's much to be famous for fine intentions, so we won't complain. Indeed, it's not our business to complain, but Posterity's; for fine intentions are really rich possessions, but they don't leave grand legacies; that is all. They mean to possess the future: they are only the voluptuous sons of the present. It's my belief, Carlino, from observation, apprehension, and other gifts of my senses, that our paternal government is not unacquainted with our intention to sing a song in a certain opera. And it may have learnt our clumsy method of enclosing names publicly, at the bidding of a non- appointed prosecutor, so to, isolate or extinguish them. Who can say? Oh, ay! Yes! the machinery that can so easily be made rickety is to blame; we admit that; but if you will have a conspiracy like a

Geneva watch, you must expect any slight interference with the laws that govern it to upset the mechanism altogether. Ah-a! look yonder, but not hastily, my Carlo. Checco is nearing us, and he knows that he has fellows after him. And if I guess right, he has a burden to deliver to one of us.'

Checco came along at his usual pace, and it was quite evident that he fancied himself under espionage. On two sides of the square a suspicious figure threaded its way in the line of shade not far behind him. Checco passed the cafe looking at nothing but the huge hands he rubbed over and over. The manifest agents of the polizia were nearing when Checco ran back, and began mouthing as in retort at something that had been spoken from the cafe as he shot by. He made a gabbling appeal on either side, and addressed the pair of apparent mouchards, in what, if intelligible, should have been the language of earnest entreaty. At the first word which the caffe was guilty of uttering, a fit of exasperation seized him, and the exciteable creature plucked at his hat and sent it whirling across the open-air tables right through the doorway. Then, with a whine, he begged his followers to get his hat back for him. They complied.

'We only called "Illustrissimo!"' said Agostino, as one of the men returned from the interior of the caffe hat in hand.

'The Signori should have known better—it is an idiot,' the man replied.

He was a novice: in daring to rebuke he betrayed his office.

Checco snatched his hat from his attentive friend grinning, and was away in a flash. Thereupon the caffe laughed, and laughed with an abashing vehemence that disconcerted the spies. They wavered in their choice of following Checco or not; one went a step forward, one pulled back; the loiterer hurried to rejoin his comrade, who was now for a retrograde movement, and standing together they swayed like two imperfectly jolly fellows, or ballet bandits, each plucking at the other, until at last the maddening laughter made them break, reciprocate cat-like hisses of abuse, and escape as they best could—lamentable figures.

'It says well for Milan that the Tedeschi can scrape up nothing better from the gutters than rascals the like of those for their service,' quoth Agostino. 'Eh, Signor Conte?'

'That enclosure about La Vittoria's name on the bills is correct,' said the person addressed, in a low tone. He turned and indicated one who followed from the interior of the caffe.

'If Barto is to be trusted she is not safe,' the latter remarked. He produced a paper that had been secreted in Checco's hat. Under the date and the superscription of the Pope's Mouth, 'LA VITTORIA' stood out in the ominous heavily-pencilled ring: the initials of Barto Rizzo were in a corner. Agostino began smoothing his beard.

'He has discovered that she is not trustworthy,' said Count Medole, a young man of a premature gravity and partial baldness, who spoke habitually with a forefinger pressed flat on his long pointed chin.

'Do you mean to tell me, Count Medole, that you attach importance to a communication of this sort?' said Carlo, forcing an amazement to conceal his anger.

'I do, Count Ammiani,' returned the patrician conspirator.

'You really listen to a man you despise?'

'I do not despise him, my friend.'

'You cannot surely tell us that you allow such a man, on his sole authority, to blacken the character of the signorina?'

'I believe that he has not.'

'Believe? trust him? Then we are all in his hands. What can you mean? Come to the signorina herself instantly. Agostino, you now conduct Count Medole to her, and save him from the shame of subscribing to the monstrous calumny. I beg you to go with our Agostino, Count Medole. It is time for you—I honour you for the part you have taken; but it is time to act according to your own better judgement.'

Count Medole bowed.

'The filthy rat!' cried Ammiani, panting to let out his wrath.

'A serviceable dog,' Agostino remarked correctingly. 'Keep true to the form of animal, Carlo. He has done good service in his time.'

'You listen to the man?' Carlo said, now thoroughly amazed.

'An indiscretion is possible to woman, my lad. She may have been indiscreet in some way I am compelled to admit the existence of possibilities.'

'Of all men, you, Agostino! You call her daughter, and profess to love her.'

'You forget,' said Agostino sharply. 'The question concerns the country, not the girl.' He added in an underbreath, 'I think you are professing that you love her a little too strongly, and scarce give her much help as an advocate. The matter must be looked into. If Barto shall be found to have acted without just grounds, I am certain that Count Medole'—he turned suavely to the nobleman—'will withdraw confidence from him; and that will be equivalent to a rope's-end for Barto. We shall see him to- night at your house?'

'He will be there,' Medole said.

'But the harm's done; the mischief's done! And what's to follow if you shall choose to consider this vile idiot justified?' asked Ammiani.

'She sings, and there is no rising,' said Medole.

'She is detached from the patriotic battery, for the moment: it will be better for her not to sing at all,' said Agostino. 'In fact, Barto has merely given us warning that—and things look like it—the Fifteenth is likely to be an Austrian feast-day. Your arm, my son. We will join you to-night, my dear Count. Now, Carlo, I was observing, it appears to me that the Austrians are not going to be surprised by us, and it affords me exquisite comfort. Fellows prepared are never more than prepared for one day and another day; and they are sure to be in a state of lax preparation after a first and second disappointment. On the contrary, fellows surprised'—Agostino had recovered his old smile again—'fellows surprised may be expected to make use of the inspirations pertaining to genius. Don't you see?'

'Oh, cruel! I am sick of you all!' Carlo exclaimed. 'Look at her; think of her, with her pure dream of Italy and her noble devotion. And you permit a doubt to be cast on her!'

'Now, is it not true that you have an idea of the country not being worthy of her?' said Agostino, slyly. 'The Chief, I fancy, did not take certain facts into his calculation when he pleaded that the conspiratrix was the sum and completion of the conspirator. You will come to Medole's to-night, Carlo. You need not be too sweet to him, but beware of explosiveness. I, a Republican, am nevertheless a practical exponent of the sacrifices necessary to unity. I accept the local leadership of Medole—on whom I can never look without thinking of an unfeathered pie; and I submit to be assisted by the man Barto Rizzo. Do thou likewise, my son. Let your enamoured sensations follow that duty, and with a breezy space between. A conspiracy is an epitome of humanity, with a boiling power beneath it. You're no more than a bit of mechanism—happy if it goes at all!'

Agostino said that he would pay a visit to Vittoria in the evening. Ammiani had determined to hunt out Barto Rizzo and the heads of the Clubs before he saw her. It was a relief to him to behold in the Piazza the Englishman who had exchanged cards with him on the Motterone. Captain Gambier advanced upon a ceremonious bow, saying frankly, in a more colloquial French than he had employed at their first interview, that he had to apologize for his conduct, and to request monsieur's excuse. 'If,' he pursued, 'that lady is the person whom I knew formerly in England as Mademoiselle Belloni, and is now known as Mademoiselle Vittoria Campa, may I beg you to inform her that, according to what I have heard, she is likely to be in some danger to-morrow?' What the exact nature of the danger was, Captain Gambier could not say.

Ammiani replied: 'She is in need of all her friends,' and took the pressure of the Englishman's hand, who would fair have asked more but for the stately courtesy of the Italian's withdrawing salute. Ammiani could no longer doubt that Vittoria's implication in the conspiracy was known.

CHAPTER XI
LAURA PIAVENI

After dark on the same day antecedent to the outbreak, Vittoria, with her faithful Beppo at her heels, left her mother to run and pass one comforting hour in the society of the Signora Laura Piaveni and her children.

There were two daughters of a parasitical Italian nobleman, of whom one had married the patriot Giacomo Piaveni, and one an Austrian diplomatist, the Commendatore Graf von Lenkenstein. Count Serabiglione was traditionally parasitical. His ancestors all had moved in Courts. The children of the House had illustrious sponsors. The House itself was a symbolical sunflower constantly turning toward Royalty. Great excuses are to be made for this, the last male descendant, whose father in his youth had been an Imperial page, and who had been nursed in the conception that Italy (or at least Lombardy) was a natural fief of Austria, allied by instinct and by interest to the holders of the Alps. Count Serabiglione mixed little with his countrymen,—the statement might be inversed,—but when, perchance, he was among them, he talked willingly of the Tedeschi, and voluntarily declared them to be gross, obstinate, offensive-bears, in short. At such times he would intimate in any cordial ear that the serpent was probably a match for the bear in a game of skill, and that the wisdom of the serpent was shown in his selection of the bear as his master, since, by the ordination of circumstances, master he must have. The count would speak pityingly of the poor depraved intellects which admitted the possibility of a coming Kingdom of Italy united: the lunatics who preached of it he considered a sort of self-elected targets for appointed files of Tyrolese jagers. But he was vindictive against him whom he called the professional doctrinaire, and he had vile names for the man. Acknowledging that Italy mourned her present woes, he charged this man with the crime of originating them: — and why? what was his object? He was, the count declared in answer, a born intriguer, a lover of blood, mad for the smell of it! — an Old Man of the Mountain; a sheaf of assassins; and more — the curse of Italy! There should be extradition treaties all over the world to bring this arch- conspirator to justice. The door of his conscience had been knocked at by a thousand bleeding ghosts, and nothing had opened to them. What was Italy in his eyes? A chess-board; and Italians were the chessmen to this cold player with live flesh. England nourished the wretch, that she might undermine the peace of the Continent.

Count Serabiglione would work himself up in the climax of denunciation, and then look abroad frankly as one whose spirit had been relieved. He hated bad men; and it was besides necessary for him to denounce somebody, and get relief of some kind. Italians edged away from him. He was beginning to feel that he had no country. The detested title 'Young Italy' hurried him into fits of wrath. 'I am,' he said, 'one of the Old Italians, if a distinction is to be made.' He assured his listeners that he was for his commune, his district, and aired his old-Italian prejudices delightedly; clapping his hands to the quarrels of Milan and Brescia; Florence and Siena — haply the feuds of villages — and the common North-Italian jealousy of the chief city. He had numerous capital tales to tell of village feuds, their date and origin, the stupid effort to heal them, and the wider consequent split; saying, 'We have, all Italians, the tenacity, the unforgiveness, the fervent blood of pure Hebrews; and a little more gaiety, perhaps; together with a love of fair things. We can outlive ten races of conquerors.'

In this fashion he philosophized, or forced a kind of philosophy. But he had married his daughter to an Austrian, which was what his countrymen could not overlook, and they made him feel it. Little by little, half acquiescing, half protesting, and gradually denationalized, the count was edged out of Italian society, save of the parasitical class, which he very much despised. He was not a happy man. Success at the Imperial Court might have comforted him; but a remorseless sensitiveness of his nature tripped his steps.

Bitter laughter rang throughout Lombardy when, in spite of his efforts to save his daughter's husband, Giacomo Piaveni suffered death. No harder blow had ever befallen the count: it was as good as a public proclamation that he possessed small influence. To have bent the knee was not afflicting to this nobleman's conscience: but it was an anguish to think of having bent the knee for nothing.

Giacomo Piaveni was a noble Italian of the young blood, son of a General loved by Eugene. In him the loss of Italy was deplorable. He perished by treachery at the age of twenty-three years. So splendid was this youth in appearance, of so sweet a manner with women, and altogether so- gentle and gallant, that it was a widowhood for women to have known him: and at his death the hearts of two women who had loved him in rivalry became bound by a sacred tie of friendship. He, though not of distinguished birth, had the choice of an almost royal alliance in the first blush of his manhood. He refused his chance, pleading in excuse to Count Serabiglione, that he was in love with that nobleman's daughter, Laura; which it flattered the count to hear, but he had ever after a contempt for the young man's discretion, and was observed to shrug, with the smooth sorrowfulness of one who has been a prophet, on the day when Giacomo was shot. The larger estates of the Piaveni family, then in Giacomo's hands, were in a famous cheese-making district, producing a delicious cheese:—'white as lambkins!' the count would ejaculate most dolefully; and in a rapture of admiration, 'You would say, a marble quarry when you cut into it.' The theme was afflicting, for all the estates of Giacomo were for the time forfeit, and the pleasant agitation produced among his senses by the mention of the cheese reminded him at the same instant that he had to support a widow with two children. The Signora Piaveni lived in Milan, and the count her father visited her twice during the summer months, and wrote to her from his fitful Winter residences in various capital cities, to report progress in the settled scheme for the recovery of Giacomo's property, as well for his widow as for the heirs of his body. 'It is a duty,' Count Serabiglione said emphatically. 'My daughter can entertain no proposal until her children are duly established; or would she, who is young and lovely and archly capricious, continue to decline the very best offers of the Milanese nobility, and live on one flat in an old quarter of the city, instead of in a bright and handsome street, musical with equipages, and full of the shows of life?'

In conjunction with certain friends of the signora, the count worked diligently for the immediate restitution of the estates. He was ably seconded by the young princess of Schyll-Weilingen,—

by marriage countess of Fohrendorf, duchess of Graatli, in central Germany, by which title she passed,—an Austrian princess; she who had loved Giacomo, and would have given all for him, and who now loved his widow. The extreme and painful difficulty was that the Signora Piaveni made no concealment of her abhorrence of the House of Austria, and hatred of Austrian rule in Italy. The spirit of her dead husband had come to her from the grave, and warmed a frame previously indifferent to anything save his personal merits. It had been covertly communicated to her that if she performed due submission to the authorities, and lived for six months in good legal, that is to say, nonpatriotic odour, she might hope to have the estates. The duchess had obtained this mercy for her, and it was much; for Giacomo's scheme of revolt had been conceived with a subtlety of genius, and contrived on a scale sufficient to incense any despotic lord of such a glorious milch-cow as Lombardy. Unhappily the signora was more inspired by the remembrance of her husband than by consideration for her children. She received disaffected persons: she subscribed her money ostentatiously for notoriously patriotic purposes; and she who, in her father's Como villa, had been a shy speechless girl, nothing more than beautiful, had become celebrated for her public letters, and the ardour of declamation against the foreigner which characterized her style. In the face of such facts, the estates continued to be withheld from her governance. Austria could do that: she could wreak her spite against the woman, but she respected her own law even in a conquered land: the estates were not confiscated, and not absolutely sequestrated; and, indeed, money coming from them had been sent to her for the education of her children. It lay in unopened official envelopes, piled one upon another, quarterly remittances, horrible as blood of slaughter in her sight. Count Serabiglione made a point of counting the packets always within the first five minutes of a visit to his daughter. He said nothing, but was careful to see to the proper working of the lock of the cupboard where the precious deposits were kept, and sometimes in forgetfulness he carried off the key. When his daughter reclaimed it, she observed, 'Pray believe me quite as anxious as yourself to preserve these documents.' And the count answered, 'They represent the estates, and are of legal value, though the amount is small. They represent your protest, and the admission of your claim. They are priceless.'

In some degree, also, they compensated him for the expense he was put to in providing for his daughter's subsistence and that of her children. For there, at all events, visible before his eyes, was the value of the money, if not the money expended. He remonstrated with Laura for leaving it more than necessarily exposed. She replied,

'My people know what that money means!' implying, of course, that no one in her house would consequently touch it. Yet it was reserved for the count to find it gone.

The discovery was made by the astounded nobleman on the day preceding Vittoria's appearance at La Scala. His daughter being absent, he had visited the cupboard merely to satisfy an habitual curiosity. The cupboard was open, and had evidently been ransacked. He rang up the domestics, and would have charged them all with having done violence to the key, but that on reflection he considered this to be a way of binding faggots together, and he resolved to take them one by one, like the threading Jesuit that he was, and so get a Judas. Laura's return saved him from much exercise of his peculiar skill. She, with a cool 'Ebbene!' asked him how long he had expected the money to remain there. Upon which, enraged, he accused her of devoting the money to the accursed patriotic cause. And here they came to a curious open division.

'Be content, my father,' she said; 'the money is my husband's, and is expended on his behalf.'

'You waste it among the people who were the cause of his ruin!' her father retorted.

'You presume me to have returned it to the Government, possibly?'

'I charge you with tossing it to your so-called patriots.'

'Sir, if I have done that, I have done well.'

'Hear her!' cried the count to the attentive ceiling; and addressing her with an ironical 'madame,' he begged permission to inquire of her whether haply she might be the person in the pay of Revolutionists who was about to appear at La Scala, under the name of the Signorina Vittoria. 'For you are getting dramatic in your pose, my Laura,' he added, familiarizing the colder tone of his irony. 'You are beginning to stand easily in attitudes of defiance to your own father.'

'That I may practise how to provoke a paternal Government, you mean,' she rejoined, and was quite a match for him in dialectics.

The count chanced to allude further to the Signorina Vittoria.

'Do you know much of that lady?' she asked.

'As much as is known,' said he.

They looked at one another; the count thinking, 'I gave to this girl an excess of brains, in my folly!'

Compelled to drop his eyes, and vexed by the tacit defeat, he pursued, 'You expect great things from her?'

'Great,' said his daughter.

'Well, well,' he murmured acquiescingly, while sounding within himself for the part to play. 'Well-yes! she may do what you expect.'

'There is not the slightest doubt of her capacity,' said his daughter, in a tone of such perfect conviction that the count was immediately and irresistibly tempted to play the part of sagacious, kindly, tolerant but foreseeing father; and in this becoming character he exposed the risks her party ran in trusting anything of weight to a woman. Not that he decried women. Out of their sphere he did not trust them, and he simply objected to them when out of their sphere: the last four words being uttered staccato.

'But we trust her to do what she has undertaken to do,' said Laura.

The count brightened prodigiously from his suspicion to a certainty; and as he was still smiling at the egregious trap his clever but unskilled daughter had fallen into, he found himself listening incredulously to her plain additional sentence:—

'She has easy command of three octaves.'

By which the allusion was transformed from politics to Art. Had Laura reserved this cunning turn a little further, yielding to the natural temptation to increase the shock of the antithetical battery, she would have betrayed herself: but it came at the right moment: the count gave up his arms. He told her that this Signorina Vittoria was suspected. 'Whom will they not suspect!' interjected Laura. He assured her that if a conspiracy had ripened it must fail. She was to believe that he abhorred the part of a spy or informer, but he was bound, since she was reckless, to watch over his daughter; and also bound, that he might be of service to her, to earn by service to others as much power as he could reasonably hope to obtain. Laura signified that he argued excellently well. In a fit of unjustified doubt of her sincerity, he complained, with a querulous snap:

'You have your own ideas; you have your own ideas. You think me this and that. A man must be employed.'

'And this is to account for your occupation?' she remarked.

'Employed, I say!' the count reiterated fretfully. He was unmasking to no purpose, and felt himself as on a slope, having given his adversary vantage.

'So that there is no choice for you, do you mean?'

The count set up a staggering affirmative, but knocked it over with its natural enemy as soon as his daughter had said, 'Not being for Italy, you must necessarily be against her:—I admit that to be the position!'

'No!' he cried; 'no: there is no question of "for" or "against," as you are aware. "Italy, and not Revolution": that is my motto.'

'Or, in other words, "The impossible,"' said Laura. 'A perfect motto!'

Again the count looked at her, with the remorseful thought: 'I certainly gave you too much brains.'

He smiled: 'If you could only believe it not impossible!'

'Do you really imagine that "Italy without Revolution" does not mean "Austria"?' she inquired.

She had discovered how much he, and therefore his party, suspected, and now she had reasons for wishing him away. Not daring to show symptoms of restlessness, she offered him the chance of recovering himself on the crutches of an explanation. He accepted the assistance, praising his wits for their sprightly divination, and went through a long-winded statement of his views for the welfare of Italy, quoting his favourite Berni frequently, and forcing the occasion for that jolly poet. Laura gave quiet attention to all, and when he was exhausted at the close, said meditatively, 'Yes. Well; you are older. It may seem to you that I shall think as you do when I have had a similar, or the same, length of experience.'

This provoking reply caused her father to jump up from his chair and spin round for his hat. She rose to speed him forth.

'It may seem to me!' he kept muttering. 'It may seem to me that when a daughter gets married—addio! she is nothing but her husband.'

'Ay! ay! if it might be so!' the signora wailed out.

The count hated tears, considering them a clog to all useful machinery. He was departing, when through the open window a noise of scuffling in the street below arrested him.

'Has it commenced?' he said, starting.

'What?' asked the signora, coolly; and made him pause.

'But-but-but!' he answered, and had the grace to spare her ears. The thought in him was: 'But that I had some faith in my wife, and don't admire the devil sufficiently, I would accuse him point-blank, for, by Bacchus! you are as clever as he.'

It is a point in the education of parents that they should learn to apprehend humbly the compliment of being outwitted by their own offspring.

Count Serabiglione leaned out of the window and saw that his horses were safe and the coachman handy. There were two separate engagements going on between angry twisting couples.

'Is there a habitable town in Italy?' the count exclaimed frenziedly. First he called to his coachman to drive away, next to wait as if nailed to the spot. He cursed the revolutionary spirit as the mother of vices. While he was gazing at the fray, the door behind him opened, as he knew by the rush of cool air which struck his temples. He fancied that his daughter was hurrying off in obedience to a signal, and turned upon her just as Laura was motioning to a female figure in the doorway to retire.

'Who is this?' said the count.

A veil was over the strange lady's head. She was excited, and breathed quickly. The count brought forward a chair to her, and put on his best court manner. Laura caressed her, whispering, ere she replied: 'The Signorina Vittoria Romana!—Biancolla!—Benarriva!' and numerous other names of inventive endearment. But the count was too sharp to be thrown off the scent. 'Aha!' he said, 'do I see her one evening before the term appointed?' and bowed profoundly. 'The Signorina Vittoria!'

She threw up her veil.

'Success is certain,' he remarked and applauded, holding one hand as a snuff-box for the fingers of the other to tap on.

'Signor Conte, you—must not praise me before you have heard me.'

'To have seen you!'

'The voice has a wider dominion, Signor Conte.'

'The fame of the signorina's beauty will soon be far wider. Was Venus a cantatrice?'

She blushed, being unable to continue this sort of Mayfly-shooting dialogue, but her first charming readiness had affected the proficient social gentleman very pleasantly, and with fascinated eyes he hummed and buzzed about her like a moth at a lamp. Suddenly his head dived: 'Nothing, nothing, signorina,' he said, brushing delicately at her dress; 'I thought it might be paint.' He smiled to reassure her, and then he dived again, murmuring: 'It must be something sticking to the dress. Pardon me.' With that he went to the bell. 'I will ring up my daughter's maid. Or Laura—where is Laura?'

The Signora Piaveni had walked to the window. This antiquated fussiness of the dilettante little nobleman was sickening to her.

'Probably you expect to discover a revolutionary symbol in the lines of the signorina's dress,' she said.

'A revolutionary symbol!—my dear! my dear!' The count reproved his daughter. 'Is not our signorina a pure artist, accomplishing easily three octaves? aha! Three!' and he rubbed his hands. 'But, three good octaves!' he addressed Vittoria seriously and admonishingly. 'It is a fortune-millions! It is precisely the very grandest heritage! It is an army!'

'I trust that it may be!' said Vittoria, with so deep and earnest a ring of her voice that the count himself, malicious as his ejaculations had been, was astonished. At that instant Laura cried from the window: 'These horses will go mad.'

The exclamation had the desired effect.

'Eh?—pardon me, signorina,' said the count, moving half-way to the window, and then askant for his hat. The clatter of the horses' hoofs sent him dashing through the doorway, at which place his daughter stood with his hat extended. He thanked and blessed her for the kindly attention, and in terror lest the signorina should think evil of him as 'one of the generation of the hasty,' he said, 'Were it anything but horses! anything but horses! one's horses!—ha!' The audible hoofs called him off. He kissed the tips of his fingers, and tripped out.

The signora stepped rapidly to the window, and leaning there, cried a word to the coachman, who signalled perfect comprehension, and immediately the count's horses were on their hind-legs, chafing and pulling to right and left, and the street was tumultuous with them. She flung down the window, seized Vittoria's cheeks in her two hands, and pressed the head upon her bosom. 'He will not disturb us again,' she said, in quite a new tone, sliding her hands from the cheeks to the shoulders and along the arms to the fingers'-ends, which they clutched lovingly. 'He is of the old school, friend of my heart! and besides, he has but two pairs of horses, and one he keeps in Vienna. We live in the hope that our masters will pay us better! Tell me! you are in good health? All is well with you? Will they have to put paint on her soft cheeks to-morrow? Little, if they hold the colour as full as now? My Sandra! amica! should I have been jealous if Giacomo had known you? On my soul, I cannot guess! But, you love what he loved. He seems to live for me when they are talking of Italy, and you send your eyes forward as if you saw the country free. God help me! how I have been containing myself for the last hour and a half!'

The signora dropped in a seat and laughed a languid laugh.

'The little ones? I will ring for them. Assunta shall bring them down in their night-gowns if they are undressed; and we will muffle the windows, for my little man will be wanting his song; and did you not promise him the great one which is to raise Italy-his mother, from the dead? Do you remember our little fellow's eyes as he tried to see the picture? I fear I force him too much, and there's no need-not a bit.'

The time was exciting, and the signora spoke excitedly. Messing and Reggio were in arms. South Italy had given the open signal. It was near upon the hour of the unmasking of the great Lombard conspiracy, and Vittoria, standing there, was the beacon-light of it.

Her presence filled Laura with transports of exultation; and shy of displaying it, and of the theme itself, she let her tongue run on, and satisfied herself by smoothing the hand of the brave girl on her chin, and plucking with little loving tugs at her skirts. In doing this she suddenly gave a cry, as if stung.

'You carry pins,' she said. And inspecting the skirts more closely, 'You have a careless maid in that creature Giacinta; she lets paper stick to your dress. What is this?'

Vittoria turned her head, and gathered up her dress to see.

'Pinned with the butterfly!' Laura spoke under her breath.

Vittoria asked what it meant.

'Nothing—nothing,' said her friend, and rose, pulling her eagerly toward the lamp.

A small bronze butterfly secured a square piece of paper with clipped corners to her dress. Two words were written on it:—

'SEI SOSPETTA.'

CHAPTER XII
THE BRONZE BUTTERFLY

The two women were facing one another in a painful silence when Carlo Ammiani was announced to them. He entered with a rapid stride, and struck his hands together gladly at sight of Vittoria.

Laura met his salutation by lifting the accusing butterfly attached to Vittoria's dress.

'Yes; I expected it,' he said, breathing quick from recent exertion. 'They are kind—they give her a personal warning. Sometimes the dagger heads the butterfly. I have seen the mark on the Play-bills affixed to the signorina's name.'

'What does it mean?' said Laura, speaking huskily, with her head bent over the bronze insect. 'What can it mean?' she asked again, and looked up to meet a covert answer.

'Unpin it.' Vittoria raised her arms as if she felt the thing to be enveloping her.

The signora loosened the pin from its hold; but dreading lest she thereby sacrificed some possible clue to the mystery, she hesitated in her action, and sent an intolerable shiver of spite through Vittoria's frame, at whom she gazed in a cold and cruel way, saying, 'Don't tremble.' And again, 'Is it the doing of that 'garritrice magrezza,' whom you call 'la Lazzeruola?' Speak. Can you trace it to her hand? Who put the plague- mark upon you?'

Vittoria looked steadily away from her.

'It means just this,' Carlo interposed; 'there! now it 's off; and, signorina, I entreat you to think nothing of it,—it means that any one who takes a chief part in the game we play, shall and must provoke all fools, knaves, and idiots to think and do their worst. They can't imagine a pure devotion. Yes, I see—"Sei sospetta." They would write their 'Sei sospetta' upon St. Catherine in the Wheel. Put it out of your mind. Pass it.'

'But they suspect her; and why do they suspect her?' Laura questioned vehemently. 'I ask, is it a Conservatorio rival, or the brand of one of the Clubs? She has no answer.'

'Observe.' Carlo laid the paper under her eyes.

Three angles were clipped, the fourth was doubled under. He turned it back and disclosed the initials B. R. 'This also is the work of our man- devil, as I thought. I begin to think that we shall be eternally thwarted, until we first clear our Italy of its vermin. Here is a weazel, a snake, a tiger, in one. They call him the Great Cat. He fancies himself a patriot,—he is only a conspirator. I denounce him, but he gets the faith of people, our Agostino among them, I believe. The energy of this wretch is terrific. He has the vigour of a fasting saint. Myself—I declare it to you, signora, with shame, I know what it is to fear this man. He has Satanic blood, and the worst is, that the Chief trusts him.'

'Then, so do I,' said Laura.

'And I,' Vittoria echoed her.

A sudden squeeze beset her fingers. 'And I trust you,' Laura said to her. 'But there has been some indiscretion. My child, wait: give no heed to me, and have no feelings. Carlo, my friend—my husband's boy— brother-in-arms! let her teach you to be generous. She must have been indiscreet. Has she friends among the Austrians? I have one, and it is known, and I am not suspected. But, has she? What have you said or done that might cause them to suspect you? Speak, Sandra mia.'

It was difficult for Vittoria to speak upon the theme, which made her appear as a criminal replying to a charge. At last she said, 'English: I have no foreign friends but English. I remember nothing that I have done.—Yes, I have said I thought I might tremble if I was led out to be shot.'

'Pish! tush!' Laura checked her. 'They flog women, they do not shoot them. They shoot men.'

'That is our better fortune,' said Ammiani.

'But, Sandra, my sister,' Laura persisted now, in melodious coaxing tones. 'Can you not help us to guess? I am troubled: I am stung. It is for your sake I feel it so. Can't you imagine who did it, for instance?'

'No, signora, I cannot,' Vittoria replied.

'You can't guess?'

I cannot help you.'

'You will not!' said the irritable woman. 'Have you noticed no one passing near you?'

'A woman brushed by me as I entered this street. I remember no one else.
And my Beppo seized a man who was spying on me, as he said. That is all
I can remember.'

Vittoria turned her face to Ammiani.

'Barto Rizzo has lived in England,' he remarked, half to himself. 'Did you come across a man called Barto Rizzo there, signorina? I suspect him to be the author of this.'

At the name of Barto Rizzo, Laura's eyes widened, awakening a memory in
Ammiani; and her face had a spectral wanness.

'I must go to my chamber,' she said. 'Talk of it together. I will be with you soon.'

She left them.

Ammiani bent over to Vittoria's ear. 'It was this man who sent the warning to Giacomo, the signora's husband, which he despised, and which would have saved him.

It is the only good thing I know of Barto Rizzo. Pardon her.'

'I do,' said the girl, now weeping.

'She has evidently a rooted superstitious faith in these revolutionary sign-marks. They are contagious to her. She loves you, and believes in you, and will kneel to you for forgiveness by-and-by. Her misery is a disease. She thinks now, "If my husband had given heed to the warning!"

'Yes, I see how her heart works,' said Vittoria. 'You knew her husband,
Signor Carlo?'

'I knew him. I served under him. He was the brother of my love. I shall have no other.'

Vittoria placed her hand for Ammiani to take it. He joined his own to the fevered touch. The heart of the young man swelled most ungovernably, but the perils of the morrow were imaged by him, circling her as with a tragic flame, and he had no word for his passion.

The door opened, when a noble little boy bounded into the room; followed by a little girl in pink and white, like a streamer in the steps of her brother. With shouts, and with arms thrown forward, they flung themselves upon Vittoria, the boy claiming all her lap, and the girl struggling for a share of the kingdom. Vittoria kissed them, crying, 'No, no, no, Messer Jack, this is a republic, and not an empire, and you are to have no rights of "first come"; and Amalia sits on one knee, and you on one knee, and you sit face to face, and take hands, and swear to be satisfied.'

'Then I desire not to be called an English Christian name, and you will call me Giacomo,' said the boy.

Vittoria sang, in mountain-notes, 'Giacomo!—Giacomo—Giac-giac-giac . . como!'

The children listened, glistening up at her, and in conjunction jumped and shouted for more.

'More?' said Vittoria; 'but is the Signor Carlo no friend of ours? and does he wear a magic ring that makes him invisible?'

'Let the German girl go to him,' said Giacomo, and strained his throat to reach at kisses.

'I am not a German girl,' little Amalia protested, refusing to go to Carlo Ammiani under that stigma, though a delightful haven of open arms and knees, and filliping fingers, invited her.

'She is not a German girl, O Signor Giacomo,' said Vittoria, in the theatrical manner.

'She has a German name.'

'It's not a German name!' the little girl shrieked.

Giacomo set Amalia to a miauling tune.

'So, you hate the Duchess of Graatli!' said Vittoria. 'Very well. I shall remember.'

The boy declared that he did not hate his mother's friend and sister's godmother: he rather liked her, he really liked her, he loved her; but he loathed the name 'Amalia,' and could not understand why the duchess would be a German. He concluded by miauling 'Amalia' in the triumph of contempt.

'Cat, begone!' said Vittoria, promptly setting him down on his feet, and little Amalia at the same time perceiving that practical sympathy only required a ring at the bell for it to come out, straightway pulled the wires within herself, and emitted a doleful wail that gave her sole possession of Vittoria's bosom, where she was allowed to bring her tears to an end very comfortingly. Giacomo meanwhile, his body bent in an arch, plucked at Carlo Ammiani's wrists with savagely playful tugs, and took a stout boy's lesson in the art of despising what he coveted. He had only to ask for pardon. Finding it necessary, he came shyly up to Vittoria, who put Amalia in his way, kissing whom, he was himself tenderly kissed.

'But girls should not cry!' Vittoria reproved the little woman.

'Why do you cry?' asked Amalia simply.

'See! she has been crying.' Giacomo appropriated the discovery, perforce of loudness, after the fashion of his sex.

'Why does our Vittoria cry?' both the children clamoured.

'Because your mother is such a cruel sister to her,' said Laura, passing up to them from the doorway. She drew Vittoria's head against her breast, looked into her eyes, and sat down among them. Vittoria sang one low-toned soft song, like the voice of evening, before they were dismissed to their beds. She could not obey Giacomo's demand for a martial air, and had to plead that she was tired.

When the children had gone, it was as if a truce had ended. The signora and Ammiani fell to a brisk counterchange of questions relating to the mysterious suspicion which had fallen upon Vittoria. Despite Laura's love for her, she betrayed her invincible feeling that there must be some grounds for special or temporary distrust.

'The lives that hang on it knock at me here,' she said, touching under her throat with fingers set like falling arrows.

But Ammiani, who moved in the centre of conspiracies, met at their councils, and knew their heads, and frequently combated their schemes, was not possessed by the same profound idea of their potential command of hidden facts and sovereign wisdom. He said, 'We trust too much to one man. We are compelled to trust him, but we trust too much to him. I mean this man, this devil, Barto Rizzo.

Signora, signora, he must be spoken of. He has dislocated the plot. He is the fanatic of the revolution, and we are trusting him as if he had full sway of reason. What is the consequence? The Chief is absent he is now, as I believe, in Genoa. All the plan for the rising is accurate; the instruments are ready, and we are paralyzed. I have been to three houses to-night, and where, two hours previously, there was union and concert, all are irresolute and divided. I have hurried off a messenger to the Chief. Until we hear from him, nothing can be done. I left Ugo Corte storming against us Milanese, threatening, as usual, to work without us, and have a Bergamasc and Brescian Republic of his own. Count Medole is for a week's postponement. Agostino smiles and chuckles, and talks his poetisms.'

'Until you hear from the Chief, nothing is to be done?' Laura said passionately. 'Are we to remain in suspense? Impossible! I cannot bear it. We have plenty of arms in the city. Oh, that we had cannon! I worship cannon! They are the Gods of battle! But if we surprise the citadel;—one true shock of alarm makes a mob of an army. I have heard my husband say so. Let there be no delay. That is my word.'

'But, signora, do you see that all concert about the signal is lost?'

'My friend, I see something'; Laura nodded a significant half-meaning at him. 'And perhaps it will be as well. Go at once. See that another signal is decided upon. Oh! because we are ready—ready. Inaction now is uttermost anguish—kills the heart. What number of the white butchers have we in the city to-night?'

'They are marching in at every gate. I saw a regiment of Hungarians coming up the Borgo della Stella. Two fresh squadrons of Uhlans in the Corso Francesco. In the Piazza d'Armi artillery is encamped.'

'The better for Brescia, for Bergamo, for Padua, for Venice!' exclaimed Laura. 'There is a limit to their power. We Milanese can match them. For days and days I have had a dream lying in my bosom that Milan was soon to breathe. Go, my brother; go to Barto Rizzo; gather him and Count Medole, Agostino, and Colonel Corte—to whom I kiss my fingers—gather them together, and squeeze their brains for the one spark of divine fire in this darkness which must exist where there are so many thorough men bent upon a sacred enterprise. And, Carlo,'—Laura checked her nervous voice, 'don't think I am declaiming to you from one of my "Midnight Lamps."' (She spoke of the title of her pamphlets to the Italian people.) 'You feel among us women very much as Agostino and Colonel Corte feel when the boy Carlo airs his impetuosities in their presence. Yes, my fervour makes a philosopher of you. That is human nature. Pity me, pardon me, and do my bidding.'

The comparison of Ammiani's present sentiments to those of the elders of the conspiracy, when his mouth was open in their midst, was severe and masterful, for the young man rose instantly without a thought in his head.

He remarked: 'I will tell them that the signorina does not give the signal.'

'Tell them that the name she has chosen shall be Vittoria still; but say, that she feels a shadow of suspicion to be an injunction upon her at such a crisis, and she will serve silently and humbly until she is rightly known, and her time comes. She is willing to appear before them, and submit to interrogation. She knows her innocence, and knowing that they work for the good of the country, she, if it is their will, is content to be blotted out of all participation:—all! She abjures all for the common welfare. Say that. And say, to-morrow night the rising must be. Oh! to-morrow night! It is my husband to me.'

Laura Piaveni crossed her arms upon her bosom.

Ammiani was moving from them with a downward face, when a bell-note of
Vittoria's voice arrested him.

'Stay, Signor Carlo; I shall sing to-morrow night.'

The widow heard her through that thick emotion which had just closed her' speech with its symbolical sensuous rapture. Divining opposition fiercely, like a creature thwarted when athirst for the wells, she gave her a terrible look, and then said cajolingly, as far as absence of sweetness could make the tones pleasant, 'Yes, you will sing, but you will not sing that song.'

'It is that song which I intend to sing, signora.'

'When it is interdicted?'

'There is only one whose interdict I can acknowledge.'

'You will dare to sing in defiance of me?'

'I dare nothing when I simply do my duty.'

Ammiani went up to the window, and leaned there, eyeing the lights leading down to the crowding Piazza. He wished that he were among the crowd, and might not hear those sharp stinging utterances coming from Laura, and Vittoria's unwavering replies, less frequent, but firmer, and gravely solid. Laura spent her energy in taunts, but Vittoria spoke only of her resolve, and to the point. It was, as his military instincts framed the simile, like the venomous crackling of skirmishing rifles before a fortress, that answered slowly with its volume of sound and sweeping shot. He had the vision of himself pleading to secure her safety, and in her hearing, on the Motterone, where she had seemed so simple a damsel, albeit nobly enthusiastic: too fair, too gentle to be stationed in any corner of the conflict at hand. Partly abased by the remembrance of his brainless intercessions then, and of the laughter which had greeted them, and which the signora had recently recalled, it was nevertheless not all in self-abasement (as the momentary recognition of a splendid character is commonly with men) that he perceived the stature of Vittoria's soul. Remembering also what the Chief had spoken of women, Ammiani thought 'Perhaps he has known one such as she.' The passion of the young man's heart magnified her image. He did not wonder to see the signora acknowledge herself worsted in the conflict.

'She talks like the edge of a sword,' cried Laura, desperately, and dropped into a chair. 'Take her home, and convince her, if you can, on the way, Carlo. I go to the Duchess of Graatli to-night. She has a reception. Take this girl home. She says she will sing: she obeys the Chief, and none but the Chief. We will not suppose that it is her desire to shine. She is suspected; she is accused; she is branded; there is no general faith in her; yet she will hold the torch to-morrow night: — and what ensues? Some will move, some turn back, some run headlong over to treachery, some hang irresolute all are for the shambles! The blood is on her head.'

'I will excuse myself to you another time,' said Vittoria. 'I love you, Signora Laura.'

'You do, you do, or you would not think of excusing yourself to me,' said Laura. 'But now, go. You have cut me in two. Carlo Ammiani may succeed where I have failed, and I have used every weapon; enough to make a mean creature hate me for life and kiss me with transports. Do your best, Carlo, and let it be your utmost.'

It remained for Ammiani to assure her that their views were different.

'The signorina persists in her determination to carry out the programme indicated by the Chief, and refuses to be diverted from her path by the false suspicions of subordinates.' He employed a sententious phraseology instinctively, as men do when they are nervous, as well as when they justify the cynic's definition of the uses of speech. 'The signorina is, in my opinion, right. If she draws back, she publicly accepts the blot upon her name. I speak against my own feelings and my wishes.'

'Sandra, do you hear?' exclaimed Laura. 'This is a friend's interpretation of your inconsiderate wilfulness.'

Vittoria was content to reply, 'The Signor Carlo judges of me differently.'

'Go, then, and be fortified by him in this headstrong folly.' Laura motioned her hand, and laid it on her face.

Vittoria knelt and enclosed her with her arms, kissing her knees.

'Beppo waits for me at the house-door,' she said; but Carlo chose not to hear of this shadow-like Beppo.

'You have nothing to say for her save that she clears her name by giving the signal,' Laura burst out on his temperate 'Addio,' and started to her feet. 'Well, let it be so. Fruitless blood again! A 'rivederla' to you both. To-night I am in the enemy's camp. They play with open cards. Amalia tells me all she knows by what she disguises. I may learn something. Come to me to-morrow. My Sandra, I will kiss you. These shudderings of mine have no meaning.'

The signora embraced her, and took Ammiani's salute upon her fingers.

'Sour fingers!' he said. She leaned her cheek to him, whispering, 'I could easily be persuaded to betray you.'

He answered, 'I must have some merit in not betraying myself.'

'At each elbow!' she laughed. 'You show the thumps of an electric battery at each elbow, and expect your Goddess of lightnings not to see that she moves you. Go. You have not sided with me, and I am right, and I am a woman. By the way, Sandra mia, I would beg the loan of your Beppo for two hours or less.'

Vittoria placed Beppo at her disposal.

'And you run home to bed,' continued Laura. 'Reason comes to you obstinate people when you are left alone for a time in the dark.'

She hardly listened to Vittoria's statement that the chief singers in the new opera were engaged to attend a meeting at eleven at night at the house of the maestro Rocco Ricci.

CHAPTER XIII
THE PLOT OF THE SIGNOR ANTONIO

There was no concealment as to Laura's object in making request for the services of Beppo. She herself knew it to be obvious that she intended to probe and cross-examine the man, and in her wilfulness she chose to be obtuse to opinion. She did not even blush to lean a secret ear above the stairs that she might judge, by the tones of Vittoria's voice upon her giving Beppo the order to wait, whether she was at the same time conveying a hint for guardedness. But Vittoria said not a word: it was Ammiani who gave the order. 'I am despicable in distrusting her for a single second,' said Laura. That did not the less encourage her to question Beppo rigorously forthwith; and as she was not to be deceived by an Italian's affectation of simplicity, she let him answer two or three times like a plain fool, and then abruptly accused him of standing prepared with these answers. Beppo, within his own bosom, immediately ascribed to his sagacious instinct the mere spirit of opposition and dislike to serve any one save his own young mistress which had caused him to irritate the signora and be on his guard. He proffered a candid admission of the truth of the charge; adding, that he stood likewise prepared with an unlimited number of statements. 'Questions, illustrious signora, invariably put me on the defensive, and seem to cry for a return thrust; and this I account for by the fact that my mother—the blessed little woman now among the Saints!—was questioned, brows and heels, by a ferruginously—faced old judge at the momentous period when she carried me. So that, a question—and I show point; but ask me for a statement, and, ah, signora!' Beppo delivered a sweep of the arm, as to indicate the spontaneous flow of his tongue.

'I think,' said Laura, 'you have been a soldier, and a serving-man.'

'And a scene-shifter, most noble signora, at La Scala.'

'You accompanied the Signor Mertyrio to England when he was wounded?'

'I did.'

'And there you beheld the Signorina Vittoria, who was then bearing the name of Emilia Belloni?'

'Which name she changed on her arrival in Italy, illustrious signora, for that of Vittoria Campa—"sull' campo dells gloria"—ah! ah!—her own name being an attraction to the blow-flies in her own country. All this is true.'

'It should be a comfort to you! The Signor Mertyrio . . .'

Beppo writhed his person at the continuance of the questionings, and obtaining a pause, he rushed into his statement: 'The Signor Mertyrio was well, and on the point of visiting Italy, and quitting the wave-embraced island of fog, of beer, of moist winds, and much money, and much kindness, where great hearts grew. The signorina corresponded with him, and with him only.'

'You know that, and will swear to it?' Laura exclaimed.

Beppo thereby receiving the cue he had commenced beating for, swore to its truth profoundly, and straightway directed his statement to prove that his mistress had not been politically (or amorously, if the suspicion aimed at her in those softer regions) indiscreet or blameable in any of her actions. The signorina, he said, never went out from her abode without the companionship of her meritorious mother and his own most humble attendance. He, Beppo, had a master and a mistress, the Signor Mertyrio and the Signorina Vittoria. She saw no foreigners: though—a curious thing!—he had seen her when the English language was talked in her neighbourhood; and she had a love for that language: it made her face play in smiles like an infant's after it has had suck and is full;—the sort of look you perceive when one is dreaming and hears music. She did not speak to foreigners. She did not care to go to foreign cities, but loved Milan, and lived in it free and happy as an earwig in a ripe apricot. The circumvallation of Milan gave her elbow- room enough, owing to the absence of forts all round—'which knock one's funny-bone in Verona, signora.' Beppo presented a pure smile upon a simple bow for acceptance. 'The air of Milan,' he went on, with less confidence under Laura's steady gaze, and therefore more forcing of his candour—'the sweet air of Milan gave her a deep chestful, so that she could hold her note as long as five lengths of a fiddle-bow:—by the body of Sant' Ambrogio, it was true!' Beppo stretched out his arm, and chopped his hand edgeways five testificatory times on the shoulder-ridge. 'Ay, a hawk might fly from St. Luke's head (on the Duomo) to the stone on San Primo over Como, while the signorina held on her note! You listened, you gasped—you thought of a poet in his dungeon, and suddenly, behold, his chains are struck off!—you thought of a gold-shelled tortoise making his pilgrimage to a beatific shrine!—you thought—you knew not what you thought!'

Here Beppo sank into a short silence of ecstasy, and wakening from it, as with an ardent liveliness: 'The signora has heard her sing? How to describe it! Tomorrow night will be a feast for Milan.'

'You think that the dilettanti of Milan will have a delight tomorrow night?' said Laura; but seeing that the man's keen ear had caught note of the ironic reptile under the flower, and unwilling to lose further time, she interdicted his reply.

'Beppo, my good friend, you are a complete Italian—you waste your cleverness. You will gratify me by remembering that I am your countrywoman. I have already done you a similar favour by allowing you to air your utmost ingenuity. The reflection that it has been to no purpose will neither scare you nor instruct you. Of that I am quite assured. I speak solely to suit the present occasion. Now, don't seek to elude me. If you are a snake with friends as well as enemies, you are nothing but a snake. I ask you—you are not compelled to answer, but I forbid you to lie—has your mistress seen, or conversed and had correspondence with any one receiving the Tedeschi's gold, man or woman? Can any one, man or woman, call her a traitress?'

'Not twice!' thundered Beppo, with a furrowed red forehead.

There was a noble look about the fellow as he stood with stiff legs in a posture, frowning—theatrical, but noble also; partly the look of a Figaro defending his honour in extremity, yet much like a statue of a French Marshal of the Empire.

'That will do,' said Laura, rising. She was about to leave him, when the Duchess of Graatli's chasseur was ushered in, bearing a missive from Amalia, her friend. She opened it and read:—

'BEST BELOVED, — Am I soon to be reminded bitterly that there is a river of steel between my heart and me?

> 'Fail not in coming to-night. Your new Bulbul is in danger. The silly thing must have been reading Roman history. Say not no! It intoxicates you all. I watch over her for my Laura's sake: a thousand kisses I shower on you, dark delicious soul that you are! Are you not my pine-grove leading to the evening star? Come, that we may consult how to spirit her away during her season of peril. Gulfs do not close over little female madcaps, my Laura; so we must not let her take the leap. Enter the salle when you arrive: pass down it once and return upon your steps; then to my boudoir. My maid Aennchen will conduct you. Addio. Tell this messenger that you come. Laura mine, I am for ever thy

'AMALIA.'

Laura signalled to the chasseur that her answer was affirmative. As he was retiring, his black-plumed hat struck against Beppo, who thrust him aside and gave the hat a dexterous kick, all the while keeping a decorous front toward the signora. She stood meditating. The enraged chasseur mumbled a word or two for Beppo's ear, in execrable Italian, and went. Beppo then commenced bowing half toward the doorway, and tried to shoot through, out of sight and away, in a final droop of excessive servility, but the signora stopped him, telling him to consider himself her servant until the morning; at which he manifested a surprising readiness, indicative of nothing short of personal devotion, and remained for two minutes after she had quitted the room. So much time having elapsed, he ran bounding down the stairs and found the hall-door locked, and that he was a prisoner during the signora's pleasure. The discovery that he was mastered by superior cunning, instead of disconcerting, quieted him wonderfully; so he put by the resources of his ingenuity for the next opportunity, and returned stealthily to his starting-point, where the signora found him awaiting her with composure. The man was in mortal terror lest he might be held guilty of a trust betrayed, in leaving his mistress for an hour, even in obedience to her command, at this crisis: but it was not in his nature to state the case openly to the signora, whom he knew to be his mistress's friend, or to think of practising other than shrewd evasion to accomplish his duty and satisfy his conscience.

Laura said, without smiling, 'The street-door opens with a key,' and she placed the key in his hand, also her fan to carry. Once out of the house, she was sure that he would not forsake his immediate charge of the fan: she walked on, heavily veiled, confident of his following. The Duchess of Graatli's house neighboured the Corso Francesco; numerous carriages were disburdening their freights of fair guests, and now and then an Austrian officer in full uniform ran up the steps, glittering under the lamps. 'I go in among them,' thought Laura. It rejoiced her that she had come on foot. Forgetting Beppo, and her black fan, as no Italian woman would have done but she who paced in an acute quivering of the anguish of hopeless remembrances and hopeless thirst of vengeance, she suffered herself to be conducted in the midst of the guests, and shuddered like one who has taken a fever-chill as she fulfilled the duchess's directions; she passed down the length of the saloon, through a light of visages that were not human to her sensations.

Meantime Beppo, oppressed by his custody of the fan, and expecting that most serviceable lady's instrument to be sent for at any minute, stood among a strange body of semi-feudal retainers below, where he was soon singled out by the duchess's chasseur, a Styrian, who, masking his fury under jest, in the South-German manner, endeavoured to lead him up to an altercation. But Beppo was much too supple to be entrapped. He apologized for any possible offences that he might have committed, assuring the chasseur that he considered one hat as good as another, and some hats better than others: in proof of extreme cordiality, he accepted the task of repeating the chasseur's name, which was 'Jacob Baumwalder Feckelwitz,' a tolerable mouthful for an Italian; and it was with remarkable delicacy that Beppo contrived to take upon himself the whole ridicule of his vile pronunciation of the unwieldy name. Jacob Baumwalder Feckelwitz offered him beer to refresh him after the effort. While Beppo was drinking, he seized the fan. 'Good; good; a thousand thanks,' said Beppo, relinquishing it; 'convey it aloft, I beseech you.' He displayed such alacrity and lightness of limb at getting rid of it, that Jacob thrust it between the buttons of his shirtfront, returning it to his possession by that aperture. Beppo's head sank. A handful of black lace and cedarwood chained him to the spot! He entreated the men in livery to take the fan upstairs and deliver it to the Signora Laura Piaveni; but they, being advised by Jacob, refused. 'Go yourself,' said Jacob, laughing, and little prepared to see the victim, on whom he thought that for another hour at least he had got his great paw firmly, take him at his word. Beppo sprang into the hall and up the stairs. The duchess's maid, ivory-faced Aennchen, was flying past him. She saw a very taking dark countenance making eyes at her, leaned her ear shyly, and pretending to understand all that was said by the rapid foreign tongue, acted from the suggestion of the sole thing which she did understand. Beppo had mentioned the name of the Signora Piaveni. 'This way,' she indicated with her finger, supposing that of course he wanted to see the signora very urgently.

Beppo tried hard to get her to carry the fan; but she lifted her fingers in a perfect Susannah horror of it, though still bidding him to follow. Naturally she did not go fast through the dark passages, where the game of the fan was once more played out, and with accompaniments. The accompaniments she objected to no further than a fish is agitated in escaping from the hook; but 'Nein, nein!' in her own language, and 'No, no!' in his, burst from her lips whenever he attempted to transfer the fan to her keeping. 'These white women are most wonderful!' thought Beppo, ready to stagger between perplexity and impatience.

'There; in there!' said Aennchen, pointing to a light that came through the folds of a curtain. Beppo kissed her fingers as they tugged unreluctantly in his clutch, and knew by a little pause that the case was hopeful for higher privileges. What to do? He had not an instant to spare; yet he dared not offend a woman's vanity. He gave an ecstatic pressure of her hand upon his breastbone, to let her be sure she was adored, albeit not embraced. After this act of prudence he went toward the curtain, while the fair Austrian soubrette flew on her previous errand.

It was enough that Beppo found himself in a dark antechamber for him to be instantly scrupulous in his footing and breathing. As he touched the curtain, a door opened on the other side of the interior, and a tender gabble of fresh feminine voices broke the stillness and ran on like a brook coming from leaps to a level, and again leaping and making noise of joy. The Duchess of Graatli had clasped the Signora

Laura's two hands and drawn her to an ottoman, and between kissings and warmer claspings, was questioning of the little ones, Giacomo and her goddaughter Amalia.

'When, when did I see you last?' she exclaimed. 'Oh! not since we met that morning to lay our immortelles upon his tomb. My soul's sister! kiss me, remembering it. I saw you in the gateway—it seemed to me, as in a vision, that we had both had one warning to come for him, and knock, and the door would be opened, and our beloved would come forth! That was many days back. It is to me like a day locked up forever in a casket of pearl. Was it not an unstained morning, my own! If I weep, it is with pleasure. But,' she added with precipitation, 'weeping of any kind will not do for these eyelids of mine.' And drawing forth a tiny gold-framed pocket-mirror she perceived convincingly that it would not do.

'They will think it is for the absence of my husband,' she said, as only a woman can say it who deplores nothing so little as that.

'When does he return from Vienna?' Laura inquired in the fallen voice of her thoughtfulness.

'I receive two couriers a week; I know not any more, my Laura. I believe he is pushing some connubial complaint against me at the Court. We have been married seventeen months. I submitted to the marriage because I could get no proper freedom without, and now I am expected to abstain from the very thing I sacrificed myself to get! Can he hear that in Vienna?' She snapped her fingers. 'If not, let him come and behold it in Milan. Besides, he is harmless. The Archduchess is all ears for the very man of whom he is jealous. This is my reply: You told me to marry: I obeyed. My heart 's in the earth, and I must have distractions. My present distraction is De Pyrmont, a good Catholic and a good Austrian soldier, though a Frenchman. I grieve to say—it's horrible—that it sometimes tickles me when I reflect that De Pyrmont is keen with the sword. But remember, Laura, it was not until after our marriage my husband told me he could have saved Giacomo by the lifting of a finger. Away with the man!—if it amuses me to punish him, I do so.'

The duchess kissed Laura's cheek, and continued:—

'Now to the point where we stand enemies! I am for Austria, you are for Italy. Good. But I am always for Laura. So, there's a river between us and a bridge across it. My darling, do you know that we are much too strong for you, if you mean anything serious tomorrow night?'

'Are you?' Laura said calmly.

'I know, you see, that something is meant to happen to-morrow night.'

Laura said, 'Do you?'

'We have positive evidence of it. More than that: Your Vittoria—but do you care to have her warned? She will certainly find herself in a pitfall if she insists on carrying out her design. Tell me, do you care to have her warned and shielded? A year of fortress-life is not agreeable, is not beneficial for the voice. Speak, my Laura.'

Laura looked up in the face of her friend mildly with her large dark eyes, replying, 'Do you think of sending Major de Pyrmont to her to warn her?'

'Are you not wicked?' cried the duchess, feeling that she blushed, and that Laura had thrown her off the straight road of her interrogation. 'But, play cards with open hands, my darling, to-night. Look:—She is in danger. I know it; so do you. She will be imprisoned perhaps before she steps on the boards—who knows? Now, I—are not my very dreams all sworn in a regiment to serve my Laura?—I have a scheme. Truth, it is hardly mine. It belongs to the Greek, the Signor Antonio Pericles Agriolopoulos. It is simply'—the duchess dropped her voice out of Beppo's hearing—'a scheme to rescue her: speed her away to my chateau near Meran in Tyrol.' 'Tyrol' was heard by Beppo. In his frenzy at the loss of the context he indulged in a yawn, and a grimace, and a dance of disgust all in one; which lost him the next sentence likewise. 'There we purpose keeping her till all is quiet and her revolutionary fever has passed. Have you heard of this Signor Antonio? He could buy up the kingdom of Greece, all Tyrol, half Lombardy. The man has a passion for your Vittoria; for her voice solely, I believe. He is considered, no doubt truly, a great connoisseur. He could have a passion for nothing else, or alas!' (the duchess shook her head with doleful drollery) 'would he insist on written securities and mortgages of my private property when he lends me money? How different the world is from the romances, my Laura! But for De Pyrmont, I might fancy my smile was really incapable of ransoming an empire; I mean an emperor. Speak; the man is waiting to come; shall I summon him?'

Laura gave an acquiescent nod.

By this time Beppo had taken root to the floor. 'I am in the best place after all,' he said, thinking of the duties of his service. He was perfectly well acquainted with the features of the Signor Antonio. He knew that Luigi was the Signor Antonio's spy upon Vittoria, and that no personal harm was intended toward his mistress; but Beppo's heart was in the revolt of which Vittoria was to give the signal; so, without a touch of animosity, determined to thwart him, Beppo waited to hear the Signor Antonio's scheme.

The Greek was introduced by Aennchen. She glanced at the signora's lap, and seeing her still without her fan, her eye shot slyly up with her shining temple, inspecting the narrow opening in the curtain furtively. A short hush of preluding ceremonies passed.

Presently Beppo heard them speaking; he was aghast to find that he had no comprehension of what they were uttering. 'Oh, accursed French dialect!' he groaned; discovering the talk to be in that tongue. The Signor Antonio warmed rapidly from the frigid politeness of his introductory manner. A consummate acquaintance with French was required to understand him. He held out the fingers of one hand in regimental order, and with the others, which alternately screwed his moustache from its constitutional droop over the corners of his mouth, he touched the uplifted digits one by one, buzzing over them: flashing his white eyes, and shrugging in a way sufficient to madden a surreptitious listener who was aware that a wealth of meaning escaped him and mocked at him. At times the Signor Antonio pitched a note compounded half of cursing, half of crying, it seemed: both pathetic and objurgative, as if he whimpered anathemas and had inexpressible bitter things in his mind. But there was a remedy! He displayed the specific on a third finger. It was there. This being done (number three on the fingers), matters might still be well. So much his electric French and gesticulations plainly asserted. Beppo strained all his attention for names, in despair at the riddle of the signs. Names were pillars of light in the dark unintelligible waste. The signora put a question. It was replied to with the name of the Maestro Rocco Ricci. Following that, the Signor Antonio accompanied his voluble delivery with pantomimic action which seemed to indicate the shutting of a door and an instantaneous galloping of horses—a flight into air, any-whither. He whipped the visionary steeds with enthusiastic glee, and appeared to be off skyward like a mad poet, when the signora again put a question, and at once he struck his hand flat across his mouth, and sat postured to answer what she pleased with a glare of polite vexation. She spoke; he echoed her, and the duchess took up the same phrase. Beppo was assisted by the triangular recurrence of the words and their partial relationship to Italian to interpret them: 'This night.' Then the signora questioned further. The Greek replied: 'Mademoiselle Irma di Karski.'

'La Lazzeruola,' she said.

The Signor Antonio flashed a bit of sarcastic mimicry, as if acquiescing in the justice of the opprobrious term from the high point of view: but mademoiselle might pass, she was good enough for the public.

Beppo heard and saw no more. A tug from behind recalled him to his situation. He put out his arms and gathered Aennchen all dark in them: and first kissing her so heartily as to set her trembling on the verge of a betrayal, before she could collect her wits he struck the fan down the pretty hollow of her back, between her shoulder-blades, and bounded away. It was not his intention to rush into the embrace of Jacob Baumwalder Feckelwitz, but that perambulating chasseur received him in a semi- darkness where all were shadows, and exclaimed, 'Aennchen!' Beppo gave an endearing tenderness to the few words of German known to him: 'Gottschaf-donner-dummer!' and slipped from the hold of the astonished Jacob, sheer under his arm-pit. He was soon in the street, excited he knew not by what, or for what object. He shuffled the names he remembered to have just heard—'Rocco Ricci, and 'la Lazzeruola.' Why did the name of la Lazzeruola come in advance of la Vittoria? And what was the thing meant by 'this night,' which all three had uttered as in an agreement?—ay! and the Tyrol! The Tyrol—this night-Rocco Ricci la Lazzeruola!

Beppo's legs were carrying him toward the house of the Maestro Rocco Ricci ere he had arrived at any mental decision upon these imminent mysteries.